Pearson Education Limited
Edinburgh Gate, Harlow,
Essex CM20 2JE, England
and Associated Companies throughout the world.

ISBN 0 582 419255

First published in the Longman Simplified English Series 1978
First published in the Longman Fiction Series 1992
This adaptation first published in 1996 by arrangement with Souvenir Press Limited
This edition first published 1999

3 5 7 9 10 8 6 4

Set in 11/14pt Bembo
Printed in Spain by Mateu Cromo, S.A. Pinto (Madrid)

Published by Pearson Education Limited in association with
Penguin Books Ltd, both companies being subsidiaries of Pearson Plc

For a complete list of the titles available in the Penguin Readers series please write to your local
Pearson Education office or to: Marketing Department, Penguin Longman Publishing,
80 Strand, London, WC2R 0RL

Contents

Introduction

Although much of his adult life was spent in North America, Arthur Hailey was born in Luton, England, in 1920, the only child of working-class parents. After leaving school at fourteen, he had a number of jobs before joining the Royal Air Force (RAF) when war broke out in 1939. His pilot training took him to the United States, and these early "insider" experiences of aviation proved useful later on in his writing. When he left the RAF in 1947 he decided to go and live in Canada where, a few years later, he became a Canadian citizen, settling in Toronto. There he worked for various magazines, but when he sold his first television play *Flight in Danger* in 1956, he felt confident that he could give up working for others and become a full-time writer. His first marriage, to Joan Fishwick in 1944, ended in divorce. It is since his second marriage to Sheila Dunlop in 1951 that he has written all his best-known works.

After the early success of *Flight in Danger*, Hailey continued to write well-received screenplays for television and film, and it was not until 1959 that he wrote his first full-length book, *The Final Diagnosis*. Hailey's strength as a storyteller is that he is concerned to present the particular worlds he deals with in his books in as realistic and detailed a manner as possible. *In High Places* (1962) is set in the world of government; *Hotel* (1965) looks behind the scenes at life in a grand hotel; air travel is the context for *Airport*; he looks at the car industry in *Wheels* (1971), at the financial world in *The Moneychangers* (1975) and at the medical world in *The Final Diagnosis* and *Strong Medicine* (1984).

Hailey has always believed in making sure that he has a thorough understanding of the background to each book, and there is no doubt that the level of detail included in his stories brings them to life in a special way. The reader is taken inside the characters, sees situations through their eyes, shares their concerns and experiences their hopes and fears. The story is carefully planned and fast-moving, and there is always a long and varied list of characters whose daily personal lives run alongside the larger emergency situation on which the story hangs. These features of Hailey's writing have made him a best-selling writer and his books are popular with readers all over the world.

He spent three years planning and writing *Airport*, one of his best works. He visited airports in North America and Europe, becoming particularly familiar with daily life at Chicago's O'Hare International Airport, one of the world's busiest air traffic centres. He spoke to all types and levels of airport employee, watched them at their work, and finally understood the special problems and responsibilities that each of them faced.

At the time the book appeared, air traffic was increasing sharply. For many people the world of aviation was still a strange and exciting one. People were discussing the subjects mentioned in the book: the problems with noise suffered by those living near airports; dangers connected with bombs; overcrowded airports and, in particular, plane crashes. In 1962, 93 people were killed in a plane crash in New York and 30 died in Kansas when their plane hit a house. Three years later 133 people died when a plane crashed in Tokyo Bay. Real-life emergencies such as these serve to heighten the tension of the story as the reader sympathizes with the ordinary characters caught up in events: the pilots and air hostesses, the airport managers and air traffic controllers, the ticket salespeople and maintenance workers. All have their personal and professional pressures and their own ways of dealing with them.

The action of the book is centred round Lincoln International Airport in Chicago, during one of the worst snowstorms to hit the city in years. The man with the responsibility for keeping the airport open is the Airport General Manager, Mel Bakersfeld.

Mel's problems are not restricted to the airport: his home life and relationship with his wife, Cindy, are also becoming extremely difficult. Fortunately he can depend on the support of some of the other people working with him, including the attractive Passenger Relations Agent, Tanya Livingston, and the strong and courageous Joe Patroni; Joe is responsible for moving a plane which is blocking the longest runway, a job that becomes more and more important as the story unfolds.

Back in Air Traffic Control, Mel's brother Keith is also facing problems. At the same time Vernon Demerest, a proud and unlikeable pilot, is doing his best to make life difficult for Mel, but is himself about to have an unpleasant surprise. People living in the Meadowood area of the city are planning a protest about the noise from the airport, encouraged by the lawyer Elliott Freemantle, who has reasons of his own for getting involved in the case. And in a cheap and dirty apartment on the south side of the city, a sad and lonely man is beginning to make plans for an event that he hopes will bring comfort to the wife he loves but can no longer support.

Chapter 1   The Storm

At half past six on a Friday evening in January, Lincoln International Airport was open, but it was having serious problems.

The airport, together with the whole of the Midwestern United States, had been hit by the worst storm in years. It had already lasted for three days. Now troubles, like spots on a sick, weakened body, were beginning to break out everywhere.

A truck carrying 200 dinners was lost in the snow somewhere on an airport service road, and so far the search for it had been unsuccessful.

At least a hundred flights were delayed, some by many hours.

Out on the airfield, runway three zero was out of use. It was blocked by an Aéreo-Mexican plane which lay sideways across it. The front wheels were stuck in the deep mud which lay under the snow near the edge of the runway. Aéreo-Mexican had tried hard for two hours to move it, but without any success. Now they were asking TWA to help them.

The loss of runway three zero made the work of Air Traffic Control even more difficult than usual. With 20 planes waiting to land, they were delaying take-offs. The airfield seemed to be full of waiting planes. Inside the main passenger terminal, too, there were crowds of impatient people waiting beside their piles of luggage. Even the large notice on the roof of the terminal – LINCOLN INTERNATIONAL AIRPORT – was hidden by the snow.

Mel Bakersfeld was surprised that the airport was still open. Mel was the Airport General Manager. He was a tall, powerful man. At the moment, he was standing by the Snow Control Desk, high in the control tower. Usually you could see the whole

1

airport from here. Only Air Traffic Control had a better view.

Tonight you could see only a few lights. This was an unusually hard winter. The storm had started five days ago in the Colorado Mountains, and then swept across a large part of the United States. It brought strong winds, freezing cold and heavy snow.

Maintenance men with snowploughs were clearing the snow as it fell, but by now many of them were terribly tired. The storm seemed to be winning.

Danny Farrow was at the Snow Control Desk, talking to the Maintenance Snow Centre by radio phone.

'We're losing ground. I need six more snowploughs out there.'

'Oh sure, sure,' an angry voice replied. 'Six more snowploughs! And where do you think they're going to come from? Any more stupid ideas?'

'We sent four ploughs out to find that truck,' Danny said. 'If they haven't found it yet, they'll just have to try harder.'

An explosion of anger came over the radio phone in reply.

Mel knew how easily tempers were lost under these conditions. These men were highly trained, and they were working as hard as they could.

The maintenance man's voice came on the phone again.

'We're worried about that truck too, Danny. The driver could freeze to death. He won't die of hunger, though, if he has any sense!'

'This search will block the service roads,' Danny told Mel. 'You'll get plenty of complaints about that.'

'I know,' Mel said. Airport managers were used to complaints. The most important thing was to save the life of the driver. For a moment, he wished that he could sit down and help Danny. Mel needed action. The cold weather was making his bad foot – an old war wound from Korea – ache. Then he realized that Danny could work better on his own.

He telephoned Air Traffic Control.

'Any progress on the Aéreo-Mexican plane?'

'Not yet, Mr Bakersfeld.'

'Is the runway still blocked?'

'Yes.'

This airport needs more runways, Mel thought. This proves it. The trouble was, there were plenty of people who disagreed with him, and they were more powerful than he was.

'And another thing,' he was told. 'As runway three zero is blocked, planes are taking off over Meadowood. The complaints have started coming in already.'

'Oh no!' Mel said. He was tired of hearing complaints from the people who lived in Meadowood. The airport had been built long before their houses, but they never seemed to stop complaining about the noise. As a result, the runway nearest to Meadowood was used only under special conditions. On the occasions when it had to be used, pilots were told to reduce the noise made by the engines on take-off. It was possible to do this, but most pilots considered it to be foolish and dangerous and hated being told to do it. In any case, it had not stopped the complaints from Meadowood.

'How many complaints have there been?' Mel asked.

'At least 50.'

'Don't they know there's a storm and we have a runway out of use?'

'We try to tell them, but they don't want to listen. I hear they're holding a meeting tonight to decide what to do next.'

More trouble, Mel thought.

He asked: 'Is my brother on duty tonight?'

'Yes.'

Mel's brother, Keith, worked in Air Traffic Control.

'Is he all right? Does he seem nervous?'

The other man paused before he replied. 'Yes, he does. More than usual. I wish I could tell him to rest, but we're short of men already.'

'I know, I know.' Recently Mel had been very worried about Keith.

He put the phone down, and thought again about a note he had received 15 minutes before. It was from Tanya Livingston. She worked for Trans America as the Passenger Relations Agent, and was a special friend of Mel's.

The note warned him that the Airlines Snow Committee, led by Captain Vernon Demerest, was going to blame Mel for the many flight delays. They were going to attack him for what they believed was bad management.

Captain Vernon Demerest was one of Trans America's most experienced pilots. He was married to Mel's sister, Sarah. The Bakersfelds were a real "aviation family", but even with this family connection Mel and Vernon were not friendly with one another. Recently they had exchanged angry words at an important meeting, and Mel felt that the critical report was a direct result of this.

He was not really worried, because he knew that he was doing everything he could to run the airport well. It was unpleasant to be criticized, but his conscience was clear.

Tanya ended her note by inviting him to have a cup of coffee with her, when he had time. Mel decided he had time now. He always enjoyed talking to Tanya.

Chapter 2   Mel Bakersfeld

Mel went down from the control tower to his office. The office was silent and empty. He took a heavy coat and boots out of a cupboard near his big desk.

He was not really on duty at the airport tonight, but because of the storm he had stayed on to help. Otherwise he would have been at home with Cindy and the children.

Or would he?

It's hard to know the truth about yourself, he thought. If there had been no storm he would probably have found some other excuse for not going home. He didn't seem to go home immediately after work very often these days. Of course, the airport kept him very busy, but – to be honest – it also offered an escape from his endless quarrels with Cindy.

Oh God! He had just noticed a note that his secretary had left on his desk, reminding him that he had promised to go to a party with Cindy that evening. Cindy hated to miss a party if she knew that any important people were going to be there.

He still had two hours. He could finish what he had to do here in time to get to the party – but he would be late.

He phoned his home number.

Roberta, his older daughter, answered.

'Hi,' he said, 'this is your Dad.'

'Yes, I know,' she said coldly.

'How was school today?'

'We had more than one class, Father. Which one are you asking me about?'

Mel sighed. There were days when he felt that his home life had become unbearable. Did all thirteen-year-old girls talk to their fathers like this? He loved both his daughters very much. There were times when he thought that his marriage had only lasted as long as it had because of them. It hurt him to hear Roberta speak so coldly. But who was to blame for her behaviour? Perhaps she had seen her parents quarrelling too often.

'Is your mother at home?' he asked.

'She went out. She hopes you'll try not to be late for the party for once.'

She was clearly repeating Cindy's words.

'If your mother calls, tell her I'll be a little late,' Mel said. There

5

was no answer, so he asked: 'Did you hear me?'

'Yes,' Roberta said. 'Have you finished? I have homework to do.'

'No,' Mel told her, 'I haven't finished. Don't talk to me like that, Roberta. I won't allow it.'

'Of course, Father.'

'And don't call me Father!'

'Yes, Father.'

Mel almost laughed, but instead he asked: 'Is everything all right at home?'

'Yes. Libby wants to talk to you.'

'In a minute. I have something else to tell you first. Because of the storm, I'll probably sleep at the airport tonight.'

Again there was no answer. Then Roberta said: 'Will you speak to Libby now?'

'Yes, please. Good night, Robbie.'

'Good night.'

The telephone changed hands, and he heard a small childish voice say: 'Daddy, Daddy! Guess what happened today!' Libby always sounded so excited with life.

'Let me think,' Mel said. 'I know. You had fun in the snow today.'

'Yes, I did. But it wasn't that.'

'Then you'll have to tell me.'

'Well, for homework we have to write down all the good things that we think will happen next month.'

She was so happy and trouble-free. Mel wondered how long she would remain like this.

'That's nice,' he said, 'I like that.'

'Daddy, Daddy! Will you help me?'

'If I can.'

'I want a map of February.'

He understood what she meant, and told her to look at the

6

calendar on his desk. He needed a map of February himself, he thought.

He heard her small feet running from the room. Someone else put the telephone down without speaking.

Mel walked out of his office carrying his coat. From here he could look down over the crowded hall of the main terminal building. He could not see a single empty seat. Every information desk was surrounded by a crowd of impatient or worried people.

The ticket agents were working under severe pressure. As he watched, one of them was speaking calmly to a young man who had lost his temper and was shouting at her. Looking down at another desk, he saw an agent quietly finding a seat on a plane for an important businessman.

Nobody looked up and saw Mel. Most passengers never gave a thought to the large number of people necessary to keep an airport running. Of course, if people knew more about the airport, they would also know more about its dangers and weaknesses. Perhaps it was better for them not to know about these things.

He walked towards Tanya's office.

'Evening, Mr Bakersfeld,' someone said. 'Are you looking for Mrs Livingston?'

'Yes, I am.'

So people were putting their names together already! Mel wondered what they were saying about his friendship with Tanya.

'She's in her office, Mr Bakersfeld. We had a little problem. She's taking care of it now.'

Chapter 3   Tanya Livingston

In Tanya's office a young girl in the uniform of a Trans America ticket agent was crying noisily.

Tanya made her sit down, and told her: 'Make yourself comfortable. We can talk later.'

For a while there was no sound in the room except the girl's crying.

Patsy Smith was about twenty. Tanya was nearer forty. Looking at the girl, she felt that the difference in their ages was even greater than that. Perhaps it was because she had been married and Patsy had not.

It was the second time that Tanya had thought about her age today. This morning she had noticed grey hairs among the red. It reminded her that she was getting older, and that by now she should know what she was doing with her life. Her own daughter was growing up.

Patsy Smith began to speak, finding the words with difficulty. Her eyes were red from crying.

'Why are some passengers so rude? I was doing my best. We all were.'

'Tell me what happened,' Tanya said.

It was a familiar story. A man had missed his flight, and it had been difficult to find him a place on another. When Patsy at last succeeded in finding him a place, he complained that he didn't want to see the film that was going to be shown on that flight, and told her that she was slow and didn't know how to do her job properly. In the end she had been unable to bear his insults any more, and she had thrown a book at him.

'Well, I hope it hit him hard,' Tanya said. 'I know how rude some people can be. Now I'm going to send you home to have a good rest.'

The girl looked up in surprise.

'Oh, I understand,' Tanya told her, 'but this mustn't happen again, Patsy, or you'll be in trouble.'

Patsy smiled weakly. 'It won't happen again, I promise.'

'Let me tell you something,' Tanya said. 'After you left, another man came and told me that he had seen what happened. He said you weren't to blame. He told me that he had a daughter the same age as you, and that he would hit anyone who spoke to her like that man spoke to you. So you see, there are some nice people in the world, after all.'

Dealing with the public could be terribly difficult, Tanya knew. It was hard to be polite when so many people were rude to you.

As Patsy was leaving the office, Mel came in.

'Have a good night's rest, and we'll expect you back tomorrow,' called out Tanya.

'I'm tired too,' Mel said. 'Will you send me home to rest?'

Tanya looked hard at him and he noticed her clear blue eyes and short red hair. She looked good in her blue uniform.

'Will you let me send you to my apartment to rest?' she asked. 'I'll cook you a good dinner.'

'I wish I could say yes, but I can't. Can I buy you a cup of coffee?'

'All right,' Tanya said, 'but I must be quick. I'm on duty for another two hours.'

As they walked towards the coffee shop, Mel said: 'Can I come to dinner some other night, Tanya? I'd like to.'

Her sudden invitation had surprised him. She had never asked him to visit her apartment before. He wondered if this could be leading to a love affair, and knew that that would be a serious matter for both of them.

'Come to dinner on Sunday,' she said.

'Thank you. I will.' Could he leave his family on a Sunday? Well, Cindy often did.

9

They had never seen the coffee shop so full of people before.

As they went to sit down, Mel almost fell, and seized Tanya's arm. I suppose people will talk about that, she thought.

'What crowds!' she remarked.

'We'll be seeing bigger and bigger crowds in the future,' Mel told her. 'We should be building bigger airports, but we're not. Some people just refuse to understand what is needed.'

He liked talking about airports and airlines to Tanya, because he knew that she was interested.

'We'll see some changes soon,' he said. 'Carrying goods by air is going to become more important than carrying passengers.'

'Oh dear,' said Tanya. 'Perhaps I'm old-fashioned, but I prefer to work with passengers.'

Mel continued to talk until a waiter came to take their order.

'Sorry, Tanya,' he said, 'I was beginning to make a speech.'

'You ought to make more speeches.'

They had first become friendly after he had made a speech to the Airport Operators' Council. Tanya had thought it a wonderful speech, and had told him so. But recently he had not been speaking in public so much.

'How did you know about the Snow Committee report?' he asked her.

'It was typed in the Trans America Office,' Tanya replied. 'I saw it there. Tell me, why does Captain Demerest dislike you so much?'

'I suppose he knows I dislike him.'

'If you want to, you can tell him that now.'

Mel turned and saw a tall, good-looking man. He was not in uniform, but he had a commanding manner. He saw Mel and Tanya, but he did not smile or speak to them.

'He's taking Flight Two to Rome tonight,' Tanya said.

Only the most experienced pilots flew Flight Two, which was called the *Golden Argosy*. Everyone knew that Vernon Demerest was a fine pilot, but few people liked him.

Mel was just thinking how attractive Tanya looked in her uniform, when she said: 'I may be out of uniform soon. I'm looking for a better post.'

'I'm sure you'll be successful,' Mel told her. 'You could get to the top in aviation if you wanted to.'

'I'm not sure if I want to,' she said slowly.

'Would you prefer to get married again?'

'How could I? Who wants a divorced woman with a child?'

Tanya's marriage had been a terrible failure. Her husband had left her before her daughter had been born.

Before they left the coffee shop, Mel phoned the Snow Desk. Danny told him that the Aéreo-Mexican plane was still stuck across the runway. Aéreo-Mexican had asked TWA for help, and TWA had sent for Joe Patroni. He was driving to the airport from his home now.

'I'm glad they sent for Patroni,' Mel said. 'If he can't move the plane, nobody can.'

There was more news. The lost truck had been found and the driver was alive and going to be all right.

'Good,' said Mel. 'I'm going out on the airfield myself in a minute.'

'Be careful,' Danny told him. 'I hear it's a bit cold out there.'

As they left the coffee shop, someone came with a message for Tanya. A stowaway had been found on a flight from Los Angeles.

'Is that all?' she said. 'That often happens.'

'Yes, but this is a very unusual kind of stowaway.'

'That might be interesting,' Mel said, 'It will give me an excuse to come and see you again later.'

Tanya touched his hand. 'Do you need an excuse?' she asked.

Chapter 4 Joe Patroni

Joe Patroni, as Mel now knew, was on his way to the airport. He had left his home, which was 25 miles from the airport, 20 minutes before, but he was making slow progress through the thick snow.

In the end the traffic stopped moving altogether. He lit a cigar.

Many stories were told about Joe Patroni.

He had begun his working life as a motor mechanic in a garage. One day he won an old plane from someone in a card game. Without any help he repaired it and taught himself how to fly it. He studied at night school and went to work for TWA as a plane mechanic.

Soon everyone knew that he was the best mechanic TWA had. Whenever there was an urgent or difficult repair job, they called Joe Patroni. He never wasted time and always told people exactly what he thought, regardless of how important the person he was talking to might be.

Now he was TWA maintenance chief at Lincoln International. He had been successful in another way, too. He had married the most beautiful air hostess in TWA. Many people were surprised when Marie married a mechanic, but now, twelve years later and with three children, they still loved one another.

Patroni waited for five minutes. Then he turned on the radio. He waited another five minutes and then decided to get out of the car.

Someone called out: 'What's happened?' and another voice replied: 'There's been an accident.'

Further along the road he found the reason for the delay. A sixteen-wheel heavy goods vehicle was lying on its side in the road. The police were trying to pull it off the road with a breakdown truck.

Patroni walked straight up to a policeman. 'You'll never move that sixteen-wheeler with one truck,' he said. 'Never in a million years.'

'Oh no?' the policeman replied. 'There's petrol on the road. You'd better put that cigar out.'

Patroni took no notice of his advice, and continued 'What you ought to do is this—'

The policeman did not need to listen for long before he realized that this man knew what he was talking about. Ten minutes later Joe Patroni was in control of the whole operation. Two more breakdown trucks were on their way, and chains were being put around the damaged vehicle.

As he worked, Patroni felt increasingly worried about the situation at the airport, where he knew that he was badly needed. But helping to clear the road, he thought, is probably the most useful thing I can do now. I can't get to the airport until the road is clear.

He stopped work to go back to his car and telephone the airport. There was a message for him from Mel Bakersfeld. Runway three zero was urgently needed.

When he left the car the snow was still falling heavily. He was glad to see that the first of the two additional breakdown trucks had arrived.

Chapter 5   The Blocked Runway

Mel went outside. His car, which had its own two-way radio, was waiting for him close by.

The strength of the wind was frightening. Freezing air came into the car through an open window, and he closed it quickly.

It was difficult to see anything, but as he drove out to the airfield Mel could see that several planes were waiting to take off. He saw the lights and the passengers sitting ready in their seats.

On his radio he heard messages passing between planes and Ground Control. The controller sounded tired, and this made him think of his brother, Keith. He hoped that he would be all right tonight.

Mel told the controller where he was going. It took him a quarter of an hour to reach the blocked runway. Out here the storm seemed to be wilder and more violent.

A shadowy figure called out to him: 'Is that Mr Patroni?'

'No,' Mel shouted, 'but he's on his way here.'

'We'll sure be glad to see him – but I don't know what he'll do. I think we've tried everything already.'

Mel asked the man his name.

'Ingram, sir,' he replied. 'I'm Aéreo-Mexican maintenance manager. At the moment I wish I had some other job.'

Ingram's face was blue with cold. He told Mel that all the passengers had been taken off the plane. It seemed to be impossible to get the plane out of the mud.

'It'll take a long time,' he said. 'Most of tomorrow, I guess.'

'It can't take a long time,' Mel said sharply. 'We need this runway quickly.'

Suddenly he shook, and not only with the cold. He had the feeling that something terrible was about to happen. He had had this feeling once before, long ago.

He went back to his car to speak to Danny Farrow.

'Where's Patroni?' he asked.

'I'll find out,' Danny promised. 'There's something else, Mel. Your wife called.'

'Did she leave a number?'

'Yes.'

'Please tell her I'll be a little late.'

Mel lit a cigarette and waited for Danny to call him back.

In a few minutes Danny told him: 'Patroni won't be here for another hour. He's stuck in the traffic. He says to tell the Aéreo-

Mexican people not to try to do anything until he arrives.'

There was another message. Cindy had phoned again. Danny didn't complain, but Mel guessed that she had been angry and had been rude to him.

Chapter 6   Vernon Demerest

Captain Vernon Demerest was 3 miles from the airport, driving his Mercedes towards a large apartment block where many of the air hostesses lived.

Parties were often held in these apartments, and love affairs between pilots and air hostesses were frequent. Vernon Demerest had had affairs with quite a large number of the beautiful and intelligent girls who lived here.

Tonight he was going to visit an attractive, dark-haired English girl. Gwen Meighen was a farmer's daughter who had come to America ten years ago, when she was eighteen. Before becoming an air hostess she had been a fashion model.

Later tonight they would fly to Rome together on the *Golden Argosy*, and spend three days in Italy before returning to the United States. They planned to go to Naples together. Vernon smiled happily as he thought of those three days. Everything was going so well for him this evening.

He had arrived at the airport early, after saying goodbye to his wife, Sarah. She was a quiet, dull woman, and in a way this was very useful to Vernon. She never asked him about his relationships with other women, and while he was married to her, no other woman could expect him to settle down with her.

Then there was the critical report the Airlines Snow Committee had made on Mel Bakersfeld. That pleased Vernon too. Now Mel would never again dare to criticize Vernon in public – as he had done recently.

15

He stopped the Mercedes outside the apartment block. He was a little early. He could imagine Naples well – a warm night, soft music, wine with his dinner and Gwen Meighen beside him. He began singing happily to himself.

Vernon would not be flying the plane himself tonight. The pilot was Captain Anson Harris, a pilot only a little less experienced than Vernon. Vernon would be checking on Harris's flying and making a report on it.

Other pilots hated being checked by Captain Demerest. He always seemed to try his hardest to find fault with them. He had already succeeded in making Captain Harris very angry, by telephoning him at home to remind him not to be late. Harris had been a pilot for 20 years, and had never once come to the airport late. Then Vernon had met him at the airport and told him that he should be wearing a TWA shirt as part of his uniform. At first Harris had thought that he must be joking. The shirts were badly made and few of the pilots wore them. In fact, he knew that Vernon himself did not wear one! When he had realized that it was no joke he had gone dark red in the face with anger, but somehow he had managed to control himself and say nothing.

Oh yes! It would be a very easy flight – for Vernon Demerest!

He knocked on Gwen's door, and then went in without waiting for an answer. Gwen was in the bathroom.

'Vernon, is that you?' she called.

Even her voice was soft and attractive. He had noticed the effect she had on passengers – especially on men.

Her clothes were laid out on the bed. She had the same uniform as all the other girls, but under it she wore underwear of the finest French silk.

'I'm glad you came early,' she called. 'I want to have a talk with you before we leave.'

'All right. We've got plenty of time.'

16

'Would you like to make some tea?'

Gwen had taught him to make tea in the English way. Sarah wondered why he drank so much tea these days!

He went into the kitchen to make the tea. He began singing again happily.

Chapter 7   Out on the Airfield

The biting wind blew across the airfield. It was as strong as ever and it drove the falling snow ahead of it.

As he drove to runway one seven, left, Mel was shaking with cold although it was warm in his car. Was he shaking just because of the cold, he wondered, or was it also because of his memories?

The pain in his foot helped to remind him of something that had happened 16 years before, when Mel had been a pilot during the Korean War.

One day he had had a strange feeling, the knowledge that something terrible was going to happen. Next day his plane was shot down into the sea. It was sinking fast and his foot was trapped. He had saved his own life by cutting at his foot with a knife. After a long time in hospital he was able to walk, but he would never be able to fly a plane again.

The strange feeling that he had had before that experience was with him again now.

Only two of Lincoln International's runways, one seven, right, and two five, were in use now. One seven, left, was being cleared and would soon be back in use. The longest and widest of the five runways was three zero, which was blocked by the Aéreo-Mexican plane.

Since the storm began, men had been working on the runways. They had to work quickly and carefully, as more than 4 inches of dry snow on the ground was dangerous for a large

17

plane. Mel wished that the public could see the way these men worked, and the great machines they used.

When he reached the men, one of them called to him: 'Why don't you join us, Mr Bakersfeld? Have a ride on a snowplough!'

Mel smiled. 'Thanks. I will.'

He climbed in beside the driver of one of the machines. He knew the man. Usually he worked as a clerk.

'How are you, Will?' Mel asked.

'Fine. A bit tired.'

'Everyone's tired. All I can say is, it can't go on for ever.'

'I like this work,' Will told him. 'It makes a change from working in the office.'

Mel understood his feeling. He too needed to get out of his office sometimes, and stand on the lonely airfield in the wind and snow. That was where he always went when he needed to think hard about something important. He had plenty to think about tonight. The airport's future, and his own.

Chapter 8   Cindy Gets Angry

Less than five years earlier the airport had been among the most modern in the world. Many people thought that it still was. They were wrong. Few people realized how old-fashioned Lincoln International had become.

Passengers usually saw nothing but the main terminal, with its bars, restaurants and shops. They did not notice that there were not enough runways. This meant that there was a take-off or a landing every thirty seconds on the two main runways, and when the airport was very busy the Meadowood situation made it necessary to use a runway which cut across one of the other two. The result was that planes were landing and taking off on flight paths which crossed one another.

The people who worked in Air Traffic Control knew exactly how dangerous this was. Only a week before Keith had said to Mel: 'There hasn't been a crash here yet, but one day there will be. I only hope that I'm not on duty when it happens.'

Now, as Mel rode in the snowplough, he watched the rapidly moving lights of a plane as it took off. Then, almost unbelievably close to the first plane, he saw more lights as a second plane landed.

'They were close,' the driver said. Frighteningly close, Mel thought.

Mel had often spoken about the need for more runways to the Airport Committee and to the City Council – the people who controlled the airport's spending. They refused to believe that a new airport had become too small so quickly.

Perhaps Keith was right, and there would have to be a big crash before they would be able to see the situation as it really was.

A decision had to be made soon, Mel knew. The airport must either look to the future or fall back into the past. The same was true of Mel himself. Only a short time ago he had been spoken of as a young man who would get to the top in aviation. Now many people doubted whether he could.

At the end of the runway he left the snowplough and drove back to the terminal in his own car. He was thinking about what had happened to him only a few years before.

He had been president of the Airport Operators' Council then, and the youngest man ever to reach that position. One day he had made a speech to the Council about the future of air transport. He had spoken of the need for good and imaginative planning in airports all over the world, and his speech had been well received in many different countries.

Next day, he was invited to the White House to meet President Kennedy. He found that he could talk easily to the

President, and that they agreed about many things. On more and more occasions the President began to ask Mel's advice about aviation. Great success seemed to be close for him.

Then President Kennedy was killed. His early death was a terrible shock to the whole nation, but Mel felt that he had lost a friend. Later he realized that the new President did not intend to ask him for advice. He was no longer the promising young man of aviation.

When he reached the terminal he spoke to Danny Farrow.

'Any news about the Aéreo-Mexican plane?'

'No, I'm afraid not.'

'Where's Joe Patroni?'

'Still on the road.'

'Let me know when he gets here,' Mel said.

'You'll be at a party, won't you?'

Mel stopped and thought. He had told Cindy that he would go to the party, but now he felt that he should stay at the airport.

'No,' he said. 'I'm not going to the party.'

'Then I think you ought to ring your wife.' Danny told him. 'I'll give you her number now.'

Mel rang her immediately. There was a moment's silence while he waited for her to come to the phone. Then he heard her voice say sharply: 'Mel, why aren't you here?'

'I'm sorry, but I couldn't leave. There've been some problems here. It's a big storm, and—'

'I don't want to listen to excuses! Just get here fast!'

Her voice was hard with anger. Mel tried to remember her as she had been before their marriage 15 years ago. Her voice had been soft and gentle then. She had been an actress, although not a very successful one. Later she liked to claim that she would have been a great success if she had not married Mel.

'I'll be at the party as soon as I can,' he told her.

'That isn't good enough. You should be here now. You

promised you would come!'

'Cindy, I didn't know there would be this storm! We have a runway out of use–'

'You have people working for you, don't you? Or are they all so stupid that you can't leave them?'

'No,' said Mel. 'They're all highly trained workers, but I'm responsible for what they do. That's my job.'

'You don't behave very responsibly to me and you're my husband. Isn't that more important?' Cindy replied.

Mel realized that she was ready to explode with anger. He pictured her looking more beautiful than ever with her big blue eyes flashing. Cindy was a very attractive woman, and anger made her more attractive. In the past their quarrels had only made him feel that he was lucky to have such a beautiful wife. But now he noticed her beauty less. She never complained about this change in him, and this made Mel think that perhaps she had found a lover. The sad thing was that he did not really care whether she had or not.

'I don't want to spoil your fun,' he told her. 'I know you like going to parties, but I don't. What I would enjoy are a few more evenings at home with the children.'

'That's not true,' Cindy said. 'And you know it.'

He felt himself grow hot with anger. He tried to control himself, but it was impossible to control Cindy. Her voice was angry but low, and Mel guessed that she didn't want the other guests at the party to hear her.

'I'll come as soon as I can,' he said again.

'Everyone else's husband is here already. Unless you intend to leave the airport immediately, please don't come at all! But if you decide not to come it will be the end for us. Do you understand me?'

'No, I don't think I do,' Mel said slowly. 'Will you tell me exactly what you mean?'

'You understand all right,' Cindy said, and put the telephone down.

As he walked back to his office, Mel's anger grew. Unlike Cindy he did not lose his temper easily, but now he was burning with anger.

He was angry not only with Cindy, but also with himself. He felt that he had failed in more than one way. He had failed to make a success of his work in aviation and of his marriage. His children would suffer because of his failures.

In his office he threw off his coat. It fell on the floor and he left it lying there. He lit a cigarette, but it tasted terrible and he put it out immediately. His foot hurt.

Long ago there had been a time when Cindy had understood his pain. She used to make him take a hot bath and try to help him to forget it. Now she would never do that again.

In sadness, he put his head in his hands.

When the telephone rang he did not hear it at first. Then he answered it. 'Bakersfeld here.'

'This is Air Traffic Control,' he heard. 'We have an emergency.'

Chapter 9 Keith Bakersfeld

Keith Bakersfeld was on duty in the Air Traffic Control radar room.

The storm was having a serious effect on radar control, although the wind and snow themselves could not be seen here. Unlike the other Air Traffic Control rooms, the radar room had no windows. The controllers worked under low lights.

Everything in the room seemed calm, but it was a false calm. Beneath it the men always lived on their nerves, and tonight the pressure on them had been increased by the storm. In the last few minutes something else had happened to increase it even more. The effect of this was like tightening a thread which is already close to breaking.

A double signal had appeared on the radar screen like a beautiful green flower. It represented a plane in trouble. This was the emergency that Mel had been told about.

The plane was a US Air Force KC-135. It was flying high above the airport in the storm, and was asking for an immediate emergency landing. Keith had seen the emergency signal appear before him on the screen. A manager had come to help him, and now both men were sending urgent messages to other controllers and by radio to other planes.

The screen they were working at was a circle of dark green glass about the same size as a bicycle tyre. It was covered with bright points of light, each of which showed the position of a plane. Tonight the screen was unusually full of these dots.

Keith was clearly very nervous. His face was thin and the green light from the screen showed the deep hollows under his eyes. During the last year or so he had changed completely in appearance and manner from a friendly, smiling person to a silent, unhappy man. He was six years younger than Mel, but he looked much older.

The men who worked with Keith had all noticed the change in him, and they knew the reason for it. They *did* care about his problems, but they had to put their own jobs first, and they had little time to help him. That was why Wayne Tevis, the manager, stayed near Keith and watched him all the time. Tevis knew that he might have to send Keith off duty early in order to rest.

He said to Keith now: 'Look, Keith, that Braniff flight is getting too close to Eastern. Turn Braniff right and then you can keep Eastern on the same course.' Keith should have seen that himself, but he hadn't.

The problem which most of the controllers were working on

was to clear a path for the Air Force KC-l35 to land. It was difficult to do this because five other planes were already circling above the airport, waiting to land. To the sides of the airport, too, other planes circled. It needed strong nerves to guide the KC-135 between all these other planes safely. To make the situation even worse, radio communication with the KC-135 had been lost.

Keith spoke. 'Braniff eight twenty-nine, make an immediate right turn.' At a moment like this a controller's voice should be calm. Keith could not control his voice, and he sounded as nervous as he was.

In another minute or two the Braniff flight would have to be turned again, and so would several other flights. This would continue until the KC-135 had been brought safely down through them. The passengers on the other planes, although they might be tired or frightened, would have to wait.

For a moment Keith wondered how the pilot of the KC-135 felt in his difficulty and danger. Lonely, probably. Keith himself was lonely. Even when he was surrounded by other people, he felt that he was alone.

He gave new paths to several flights. Behind him he could hear Wayne Tevis trying to reach the KC-135 by radio, with no success. The green signal on the screen showed that the pilot was doing the right thing. He must know that his position could be seen on the radar screen, and that the controllers would clear a path for him.

All around him Keith could hear low voices. Everyone was working to the limits of their strength and abilities. A controller had to hold so much in his mind. Even the best controller knew that one day he might make a mistake, with terrible results.

Keith had been one of the best controllers. Until a year ago others had asked him for help and advice. Now he had to accept help from them. He must not make any mistakes tonight.

Nobody knew, not even his wife, Natalie, but this was the last time Keith would ever sit in this radar room. It was also the last day of his life.

'All right, Keith,' Tevis said. 'Go and take a break.'

Keith knew that the time for his break was not for another half an hour. Tevis did not trust him. Should he argue with him? No, Tevis was right not to trust him.

He waited for a few minutes while the man who would take his place studied the screen. The effort needed was enormous. As a result of this many controllers suffered from bad health. Others became very short-tempered, and many found that their marriages ended in divorce.

As Keith left the room, Tevis told him: 'Your brother said he might come and see you later.'

Keith was glad to be alone now. He wanted a cup of coffee and a cigarette. He went to the small rest room used by the controllers. Now that he had a few minutes to think clearly, he hoped that the KC-135 would be brought down safely.

He lit a cigarette and took out some food which Natalie had prepared for him. Sometimes she put a little note in with the food. She tried hard to make him laugh and to help him through his troubles. But recently her eyes had been red from crying and she had written fewer notes. Perhaps she knew that it was hopeless.

He wanted to help her, but how could he when he could not help himself? He had a photograph of her in his pocket, showing her on holiday in Canada, happy and smiling. She loved him, he knew. He tried to love her, but he had no love left now, only hopelessness.

Mel, too, loved Keith as much as any brother could, but he could not help him either. Nobody could help Keith now.

He opened the bag of food. No note today. It was better this way, really. Natalie knew nothing about what he planned to do.

When he came off duty at the airport he would go to a hotel where he had taken a room. The room key was in his pocket. He took it out to check.

Chapter 10 The Meeting in Meadowood

The information which Mel Bakersfeld had been given about a meeting in Meadowood was quite correct.

The meeting had started half an hour earlier in a church hall. It had started late because the 600 people who had come had to fight their way to it through thick snow. But they had come.

They were the sort of people you would find in any small town. An equal number of men and women were present. As it was Friday night, most of them were dressed informally. Several newspaper reporters were also there.

The room was uncomfortably crowded and full of smoke. All the chairs were taken, and at least a hundred people were standing.

Only an extremely serious matter could have brought them out from their warm homes on such a terrible night. They were all, at the moment, extremely angry.

They were angry for two reasons. First, because of the noise which could be heard night and day in their homes, and second, because even during this meeting the noise of planes taking off was making it impossible for them to hear one another. In fact, it was unusually noisy tonight. Of course, they did not know that this was because runway three zero was blocked by the Aéreo-Mexican plane, so that runway two five was being used. This was the runway nearest to Meadowood.

During a short silence, the red-faced chairman announced loudly that it was impossible to live in such terrible conditions.

'We have tried to reason with the airport management,' he

shouted, 'but they take no notice of our suffering.'

The chairman was Floyd Zanetta, the sixty-year-old manager of a printing company. Near him sat a younger man, a lawyer called Elliott Freemantle.

'What do the airport and airlines do?' Zanetta shouted. 'I'll tell you! They pretend to listen to us. They make empty promises to us. They are nothing but cheats and liars!'

The word 'liars' was lost in a sudden, almost unbelievable burst of sound. The room shook, and a glass of water on a table near Zanetta almost fell to the floor. The noise ended as suddenly as it had begun. This had been happening since the beginning of the meeting.

Zanetta continued. 'As I said, they are cheats and liars. I think what is happening now proves it, and—'

'Mr Chairman,' a woman's voice interrupted, 'we've heard all this before. What I and all the others here want to know is what we can do about it!'

'If you'll kindly let me finish—' Zanetta said. He never did. Once again, the terrible noise exploded over them. Some people even began to laugh, and Zanetta looked hopelessly around him.

He began to speak again, telling the people of Meadowood that they could not afford to be polite any longer. He had brought Elliott Freemantle, a lawyer who had made a special study of cases like theirs, to give them some good advice.

He talked on and on. Elliott Freemantle was getting restless.

He wanted the old fool to stop talking and sit down. Elliott had taken care to dress well and expensively for this meeting. He knew that people liked their lawyers to look successful.

He was hoping to become even more successful over this airport business. Few of Elliott's colleagues believed that he knew much about law, but they all had to admit that he knew how to make money. In fact he had made no special study of noise problems, but he was clever enough to have made Zanetta believe that he knew all about the subject.

Thank God! Zanetta had finished at last! Before he had even had time to sit down, Elliott was on his feet and talking.

'If you're expecting me to be kind and understanding, you can go home now,' he began roughly. 'I'm not offering you my shoulder to cry on. My business is law, and nothing but law.'

This speech made everyone look up. He saw that he had their attention. The reporters began writing busily.

'I have no interest in your personal problems,' he told them. 'My only aim is to see that justice is done. I'm selfish and I'm single-minded, but I'll be able to help you where a nice understanding lawyer would fail.'

He watched their faces closely as he spoke. He had guessed correctly that they were tired of words and ready for action. He noticed a man who was whispering to his wife, and guessed from the expression on his face that he was saying: 'This is what we wanted to hear.'

'Now listen,' Elliott said. 'I'm going to talk about your problem.'

He told them that laws about noise were changing fast. In many recent cases it had been proved that an airport could be taken to court by ordinary people just like the people who lived in Meadowood. And they could win, too. An airport could be forced to pay them a large amount of money. He did not tell them how rarely this happened, and how often people lost such cases. In fact, he didn't really care whether they won or lost their case. He thought that they would probably lose – if the case ever reached the courts at all. What he wanted was the money they would pay him. He had already calculated that he could make twenty-five thousand dollars out of these people. All that they had to do was to sign a paper which named him as their lawyer.

He finished his speech with these words: 'There is no time left for anything but action. Action now!'

A young man who was sitting near the front of the hall sprang to his feet. 'Tell us what to do!' he shouted.

'You must start – if you want to – by signing this paper.'

'Yes, we want to,' several hundred voices replied.

The meeting had been a great success, just as Elliott Freemantle had expected it to be.

He had promised them action, and that was what they would get. The action would begin at the airport. Now. Tonight.

Chapter 11 A Ruined Man

At the same time that Elliott Freemantle was enjoying his success, a former builder called D. O. Guerrero was tasting the bitterness of failure.

He was about 15 miles from the airport, in a locked room in a poor, dirty apartment on the south side of the city. The apartment was above an evil-smelling eating house.

D. O. Guerrero was a thin, sickly sort of man, with an unhealthy, yellowish face, deep hollows around his eyes and pale, thin lips. He was losing his hair. He had nervous hands, and could not keep his fingers still. He smoked continuously, lighting a fresh cigarette from the end of each old one. He needed a wash and a clean shirt. He was fifty, but he looked several years older.

He was married, and had been for 18 years. In some ways it had been a good marriage. He and Inez accepted one another, and their married life had been calm and uneventful. D. O. had always been too busy to be interested in other women. But in the last year he and Inez had grown apart. He could no longer share his thoughts with her. This was one of the results of a number of business failures which had made the Guerrero family poor. They had been forced to leave their comfortable home and to move to cheaper and cheaper apartments, and in the end to this dark and dirty hole.

Inez did not enjoy living like this, but she would have been able to bear it if her husband had not become so strange and bad-tempered recently. At times it was impossible to talk to him. A few weeks ago he had hit her across the face, hurting her badly. He refused to show any sorrow or even talk about it later. After that, Inez had sent their two children – a boy and a girl – to stay with her married sister, and had taken a job in a coffee shop. She had to work hard, and did not earn much, but they needed the money for food. D. O. hardly seemed to notice that the children had gone.

Inez was at work now. D. O. was alone in the apartment. Like a number of other people, he was about to leave for the airport. In his coat pocket he had a ticket for Trans America Flight Two to Rome. Inez did not know anything about the ticket or why her husband had bought one.

The ticket cost four hundred and seventy-four dollars. D. O. had paid forty-seven dollars and had promised to pay the rest over the next two years. It was highly unlikely that the money would ever be paid. He had got the forty-seven dollars by selling his wife's last possession, her mother's ring.

Only an airline would have been foolish enough to sell a ticket to D. O. Guerrero in this way. Airlines were very ready to lend money – perhaps because most of the people who bought tickets from them were so honest.

Guerrero was a ruined man. There was no money to pay what he owed. He would probably be sent to prison if the police ever found out about some of his business deals. He did not even have the money to pay the rent on this cheap apartment. Soon he and Inez would be homeless. He could see no future for them.

His plan was to blow up Trans America Flight Two. He himself would die, but he did not care about that. His life was of no value now to himself or his family, but his death would be of great value. He had decided to take out life insurance for seventy-five thousand dollars, and to save his family from ruin by his death.

In his hopelessness he had no thought or pity for all the people who would die with him. He believed that he was acting out of love for his family.

He had been thinking about his death for several months now. He believed that his plan was perfect. He had made a study of such cases, and intended to learn by the mistakes other people had made. The plane must disappear completely. Four hours after take-off it would be high above the Atlantic Ocean. If it exploded there, the pieces would be lost in the sea. Nobody would ever be able to find out the truth about how the crash had happened.

Guerrero had made a simple but deadly bomb, small enough to put into a little, flat case that he could carry with him onto the plane. He had only to put his hand into the case and pull a string. It would all be over in a second. The public did not know how easy it was to make a bomb. As a builder, Guerrero had often used explosives, and he had no difficulty in finding what he needed.

He hid the bomb under some clothes and papers in the case and looked at the clock. Two hours before take-off. Time to go to the airport. He had just enough money to get there and to buy the insurance policy.

One last thing! A note for Inez. He thought for a few seconds and then wrote: "I won't be home for a few days. I'm going away. I expect to have some good news soon, which will surprise you." He signed it "D. O."

He paused. It seemed so little to say after 18 years of marriage, but it would be dangerous to say more. The police were certain to examine the note later. He left it on the table.

As he went out, he could hear music and laughter coming from downstairs. It was still snowing.

Chapter 12   Joe Patroni Clears the Road

Once again Joe Patroni returned to his warm car and telephoned the airport. He reported that the road to the airport was still closed, but that it would be possible to move the heavy vehicle that was blocking it. He was told that the Aéreo-Mexican plane was still across the runway, and that everyone was calling for him to come and help them to move it.

He hurried back to the group of people around the crashed goods vehicle. It lay on its side, covered with snow now, like a huge dead animal. Three more breakdown trucks had arrived, as Patroni had requested. Their lights shone on the white snow and made it as bright as day.

Some television cameramen had also arrived, and were behaving as if the accident had been arranged specially for them. Everything would have to wait until they had got some good pictures on film.

When Patroni had gone to phone the airport, he had left the breakdown trucks in the best positions to pull the crashed sixteen-wheeler off the road. Chains were being put around it. When he came back, the chains had gone and the trucks were in a different place. A crowd of people had come to watch the television cameras.

Wet snow had got inside the collar of Patroni's coat. It was uncomfortable, and it added to his anger. He rushed up to a policeman and demanded: 'Who took the chains off the sixteen-wheeler? And what fool moved the breakdown trucks? Where they are now, they're useless!'

'I know,' the policeman said, 'but they'll look better on television like this.'

Patroni remembered the serious situation that was waiting for him at the airport, and felt ready to break the television cameras. He was strong enough to do it, too. He had a hot, violent temper, but he had learned to control it long ago.

In his youth he had killed a man in a boxing match. Since then he had been careful to control himself. These days he reasoned with people instead of hitting them.

He told the policeman who was in charge of the operation: 'You've just blocked the road for a further 20 minutes, playing the fool with those television cameras. I told you, there's an emergency at the airport. Now listen to this! I've got a phone in my car, and I can tell my chief at the airport what you're doing. If he passes on the information to your chief you may be in big trouble, my friend.'

For a moment, the policeman looked as if he was going to shout at Patroni. Then he turned to the cameramen and shouted: 'OK, no more filming! Get those cameras out of the way!'

He had realized that Joe Patroni knew what he was talking about. He let Patroni direct the operation, and soon the breakdown trucks were pulling the heavy goods vehicle off the road. Snowploughs moved in quickly to clear the snow away.

The distant sound of a plane reminded Patroni of what he had to do at the airport. He started to walk back to his car.

'Thanks a lot!' the policeman called after him.

Chapter 13   Gwen

Captain Vernon Demerest whistled in surprise when he saw what was inside Gwen's kitchen cupboard. He had been looking for some teacups, and instead he had found a cupboard full of bottles. All of them had airline names on them. There were about 300, he calculated.

'I've got some more in the bedroom.' Gwen's voice said brightly from behind him. 'They're for a party. I think this will be enough, don't you?'

She had come into the kitchen quietly, and he turned around to look at her. Every time he saw her he thought again how lucky he was, although he was used to success with women. Her uniform made her look very young, and her black hair and dark eyes shone under the kitchen light. She smiled at him.

'You can kiss me,' she said. 'I haven't put on my make-up yet.'

He put his arms around her and kissed her. After a few moments, she pushed him away.

'I want to talk to you,' she said firmly.

She turned to close the cupboard door.

'Wait a minute, Gwen!' Vernon cried. 'What about all those bottles?'

'Well, the passengers didn't drink them, so they will be useful for my party. I've been collecting bottles off flights for a long time for a special occasion.'

Seeing his face, she continued: 'Don't look so disapproving. All the girls do it. It isn't stealing, you know.'

Vernon had heard before that a clever air hostess could live cheaply off the food that the passengers didn't want. Some of their apartments were full of things like airline cups and glasses, too. But he had never seen so much airline property in a girl's apartment before. He had to laugh.

'You'll come to the party, won't you?' Gwen asked.

'If I'm invited.'

'Of course you are.'

They sat down in the kitchen and she poured the tea – into airline cups. She did it beautifully, as she did everything.

Vernon was still thinking about all those bottles, when her voice interrupted his thoughts.

'What I have to tell you, Vernon, is that I'm going to have a baby.'

For a moment he could not believe his ears.

'You're what?'

'I'm going to have a baby,' she repeated calmly.

'Are you sure?'

She laughed and drank a little tea. He felt that she was laughing at him. He also felt that she had never looked so beautiful before.

'Of course I'm sure. I wouldn't tell you otherwise. More tea?'

'No!'

There was a silence before he said: 'I don't know how to ask you this, but . . .'

'You must ask,' Gwen said, looking at him with her big, honest eyes. 'You want to know if I'm sure that it's your child, don't you?'

'Yes, I'm sorry, Gwen.'

'Don't be sorry,' she said. 'I want to tell you.' She was speaking quickly now, and did not sound so calm. She looked down.

'There hasn't been anybody else. There couldn't be. You see – I love you. I've loved you for quite a long time now.'

Vernon took her hands gently in his. 'Listen to me. We have plans to make.'

Now that the first shock was over, he was thinking about what they would have to do.

'You don't have to do anything,' Gwen said. 'I intend to look after myself. I had to tell you because the baby is yours and you have the right to know about it.'

'Of course you must allow me to help you,' he said.

She could either give the baby away or have an abortion. An abortion would be the best solution to the problem. He would pay, of course. After all, he wasn't irresponsible. But how annoying! He needed all his money at the moment for some work he was having done on the house.

He asked: 'You're still coming to Naples with me?'

'Of course. I've been looking forward to it. Don't you believe I love you? Do you love me?'

He kissed her. 'Yes, I love you.' It was true, he thought – at the moment.

As they drove off to the airport in his Mercedes, he told her: 'You really mustn't worry, Gwen. This happens to lots of girls. I suppose you know all about the Three Point Plan?'

'I've heard of it, of course.'

The Three Point Plan was the name given to the airlines' way of helping an air hostess in her situation. The airline paid for the girl to take a "holiday". The baby would be given away soon after its birth, and she would never see it again. She had to tell the airline the father's name, and he was asked to help pay her medical bills. Later, she could return to her job.

Vernon told Gwen all the details of the plan.

'How do you know so much about this?' she asked.

'Oh, everybody knows about these things.'

'Not all the details,' she said. 'Vernon, this has happened to you before, hasn't it?'

He paused, and then admitted: 'Yes, it has.'

'How many times?' she asked. Her voice was bitter.

'Only once.'

'What happened to the baby?'

'It was given away.'

'Was it a boy or a girl?'

'I think it was a girl.'

'You *think* it was a girl? Don't you know?'

'It was a girl.'

He didn't want to talk about his daughter. He had never seen her.

'Thank you for telling me the truth,' Gwen said.

He took her hand. 'We'll have a great time in Naples, I promise you.'

He almost wished that he could divorce Sarah and marry Gwen – but that would be stupid. He had seen too many other men of his age make fools of themselves over young women. It usually ended badly. He had failed so far to talk to Gwen about the possibility of an abortion. He must do that later. As they drove into the airport he realized that now he had to think about the flight to Rome, and nothing else.

Chapter 14   Keith Remembers

The key was to Room 224 of a hotel near the airport.

Standing in the small rest room near the air traffic radar room, Keith Bakersfeld realized that he had been looking at the key for several minutes. Or was it only a few seconds? Recently he seemed to have lost all sense of time. Natalie had found him more than once just standing still and looking at nothing. He supposed that his brain was like a worn-out motor that was no longer working properly.

The human brain could do wonderful things. It could produce great works of art and science. It could also keep alive the pain of memories that a man would prefer to forget. Keith had memories that he could never forget. Only his death, which he had decided would take place tonight, would end his suffering.

He must go back to the radar room now and finish his duty. That seemed to be the right thing to do. Then he would go to the hotel and swallow a large amount of Nembutal. Enough to make him go to sleep and never wake up again.

He looked at the key. Room 224. The number reminded him of what had happened on June 24th a year and a half ago. It was the beginning of his pain, and the reason he would die tonight.

June 24th had been a beautiful summer's day, with a clear blue sky and hardly a cloud in sight. Keith had felt happy and lighthearted as he drove to work. He was not working at Lincoln International then, but at the Washington Air Traffic Control Centre in Leesburg.

Even inside the radar room, which had no windows, he felt the beauty of the summer's day.

The Leesburg Centre was not near an airport, but it was one of the busiest air traffic control centres in the country. Helped by a man called Perry Yount, Keith controlled traffic in the Pittsburgh–Baltimore area. There was also another young controller, George Wallace, who was being trained by Keith.

He went into the control room and looked at the screen. It was quite busy. Perry Yount had some additional work to do today, and left Keith to work alone with George Wallace. George would finish his training and become a full controller in only one week from now. Keith allowed him to give directions to two planes which were coming too close to one another, and saw that he was making the correct decisions. Keith was a successful teacher, and he was proud of Wallace's progress.

From time to time Perry Yount came to see if Keith and Wallace needed any help. Everything was going well. Then, just before 11 o'clock, Keith had to go to the washroom. Perry Yount agreed to stay near Wallace until he returned.

Keith stayed a long time in the washroom. It had a window, and he could look out and see green fields and flowers. It was a hot day, and he felt that he would rather go out into the fresh air than back into the control room. He often felt like this.

◆

After Keith had left, Perry Yount had an emergency to deal with. A passenger on a plane had had a heart attack. He had to clear a way for the plane to land at Washington.

◆

In the washroom, Keith wondered how much longer he could keep doing this job. He was very tired. He was thirty-eight, and had been a controller for 15 years. He felt that he was getting old.

Doctors knew that controllers became ill more often than people in less responsible jobs. Few other jobs put so much pressure on a man, and for many it was too much. They often found it difficult to sleep, and suffered from nervous diseases. Some controllers were like old men at the age of forty-five.

He looked out of the window again. If only he could go out! But he had to go back to the control room. He would go back – in a minute.

◆

Perry Yount was bringing the plane down safely over Washington, changing the courses of 15 other planes in order to clear a path for it. He handled the emergency well, as he always did. Whenever he had a free moment, he checked that George Wallace was all right. He seemed to be. Keith would soon be back to help them.

Keith was still at the window. He was thinking now of Natalie. They had started to quarrel recently, for the first time. She wanted him to save his health by changing his job. But how could he? This was the only job that he knew how to do.

◆

High above West Virginia, Irving Redfern was flying his small private Beech Bonanza to Baltimore. With him were his wife, Merry, and their two children, Jeremy and Valerie. Wallace saw the Redfern's plane as a small green dot among the larger dots of airline planes. Redfern was following a safe course.

But there was something that neither Yount, Wallace nor Redfern knew. An Air National Guard T-33 trainer was flying in the area. The pilot, Captain Neel, was experienced but careless.

Without realizing it, he had wandered a long way off course. His plane appeared as a dot on the edge of George Wallace's screen. Wallace did not notice it.

◆

A man can't just leave his job, Keith was thinking. Not if he has a wife and children to look after. Unlike pilots, controllers did not earn a lot of money. But he couldn't leave the safety of a job he knew he was good at. He would have to talk to Natalie again. Looking at his watch, he realized that he had been in the washroom for 15 minutes. He must have been dreaming! He hurried back to the control room.

As he came in he noticed that everyone was busier than before. He looked at the screen.

'What's the other traffic near the Beech Bonanza?'

'What other traffic?'

Then Wallace saw the fast-moving dot on the edge of the screen. 'Oh my God!' he cried out.

With a single rapid movement Keith pushed him to one side and seized control. He shouted to Irving Redfern: 'Make an immediate right turn *now*!'

Captain Neel's plane was rushing towards the Beech Bonanza.

If Irving Redfern had acted immediately, he might have saved himself and his family. He was a good pilot, but not a professional, and he was a polite man who always thought before he acted. Now he wasted the few seconds he had by replying to Keith's message.

In the control room they watched in silence, praying hard, as the bright green dots flew towards one another.

'Washington Centre, this is Beech–' they heard, and then the voice suddenly stopped.

The dots on the screen met, and up in the clear blue sky the Beech Bonanza was falling, spinning wildly, to the earth.

Then the terrible thing happened, the thing that Keith would never forget. The radio of the Beech Bonanza was still working. The cries of the Redfern family were heard clearly in the control room, and the voice of nine-year-old Valerie was especially clear. All over the control room faces turned white, and George Wallace broke down and cried as he heard her cries of terror. 'Daddy! Do something! I don't want to die! I don't want to die!'

The small plane crashed and burned with the Redferns inside it. Captain Neel landed safely by parachute, 5 miles away.

◆

Perry Yount was blamed for the crash, and he lost his job. George Wallace could not be held responsible, but he could never now work as a controller. They were both ruined men. Yount had to go into hospital, and then, began to drink heavily.

Keith was not blamed in any way for the crash, but he knew in his heart that he was responsible. If he had not stayed in the washroom for so long on that lovely summer's day, the Redfern family would still be alive.

He got little sleep, and when he did sleep he had terrible dreams. They always ended with the hopeless cries of little Valerie Redfern. Sometimes he tried to stay awake, so that he would not dream of her again. During the day, too, he thought about her. He could not look at his own two healthy children without feeling guilty.

His work suffered. He lost the ability to make quick decisions. Natalie begged him to change his job. Once, almost crying, she told him that unless he did something she would take the children away from him, because she could not bear to see them growing up in such an unhappy home.

It was then that Keith first thought of killing himself.

He put his hand in his pocket and touched the key again. He would need it soon.

41

Chapter 15   The Stowaway

It was almost an hour since Tanya had left Mel. She remembered his words: 'It will give me an excuse to come and see you again.'

She knew that he had to go to a party with his wife, but she hoped that he would come and see her before he left.

The 'excuse' that he had spoken of was his interest in the message received by Tanya while in the coffee shop. The stowaway was with Tanya now. A little old lady from San Diego. She was wearing a black dress, and looked like somebody's grandmother on her way to church.

'You've done this before, haven't you?' Tanya asked her.

'Oh yes, my dear. Quite a few times.'

She sat there looking quite untroubled by her conscience.

Tanya wondered if many people realized how many stowaways there were on planes these days. Probably not. Airlines tried to keep quiet about it.

The old lady's name was Mrs Ada Quonsett, and she would certainly have reached New York if she had not made one mistake. She had told her secret to another passenger, who had told an air hostess.

'All right,' Tanya said. 'I think you'd better tell me all about it.'

'Well you see,' the old lady began, 'My husband's dead, and I have a married daughter in New York. Sometimes I get lonely, and I want to visit her. So I go to Los Angeles and get on a plane to New York.'

'Without a ticket?'

Mrs Quonsett looked surprised. 'Oh my dear, I couldn't possibly afford a ticket. It's difficult enough for me to find the money to get to Los Angeles on the bus.'

'Do you pay for the bus ticket?'

'Oh, yes. They always check the tickets on the bus.'

'Why don't you fly from San Diego?' Tanya asked.

'I'm afraid, my dear, they know me there.'

'You mean you've been caught at San Diego?'

'Yes,' the old lady said quietly.

'Have you been a stowaway on many different airlines?'

'Oh yes, but I like Trans America best.'

Tanya wanted to laugh. She could hardly believe her ears. 'Why do you like Trans America, Mrs Quonsett?' she asked.

'Well, they're always so nice to me in New York. After I've stayed with my daughter for a week or two and I want to go home, I go to the airline offices and tell them.'

'You tell them the truth? That you came to New York as a stowaway?'

'Yes, my dear, of course.'

Tanya was amazed. 'And what happens then?'

The old lady looked surprised. 'Nothing happens. They send me home. Sometimes they get a bit angry and tell me not to do it again, but that isn't much, is it?'

'No,' Tanya said, 'it certainly isn't.'

The really unbelievable thing, she thought, was that it was all true. Airlines knew that it often happened. They also knew that it cost more to delay a flight in order to check the passengers than to allow an occasional stowaway to travel free.

'You're nice,' Mrs Quonsett said. 'You're a lot younger than most of the airline people I've met. You must be about twenty-eight.'

'Thirty-seven.' Tanya said sharply.

'Well, you look very young. Perhaps it's because you're married.'

'Stop it,' Tanya told her. 'It isn't going to help you.'

'But you are married.'

'I was. I'm not now.'

'What a pity. You could have beautiful children with red hair like your own.'

Red, Tanya thought, not grey – the grey that she had noticed that morning. She had a child, anyway. Her daughter was at home now, sleeping.

'You've broken the law,' she told Mrs Quonsett. 'I suppose you realize that you could be charged?'

'But I won't, will I?' replied the old lady, smiling. 'The airline won't do anything. They never do.'

Tanya knew that it was true.

'You've had a lot of free travel from Trans America, Mrs Quonsett,' she said. 'Now I'd like you to help us a little.'

'I'll be glad to if I can.'

She asked Mrs Quonsett to tell her how she got on to flights without a ticket. The old lady knew a surprising number of tricks.

When she had finished, Tanya said: 'You seem to have thought of everything!'

'My husband taught me to be thorough,' Mrs Quonsett replied. 'He was a teacher, and an extremely thorough man himself.'

The telephone rang. It was the Transport Manager.

'Have you spoken to the old woman yet?' he asked Tanya.

'Yes. She's with me now.'

'Did she tell you anything useful?'

'Yes, I'll send you a report. And I need a ticket to Los Angeles for her. We'll send her back tonight.'

'I hate to put her before all the honest passengers,' the manager said, 'but I suppose we'll have to.'

The old lady had one more important thing to tell Tanya.

'It's best not to take a direct flight,' she said. 'They get rather full, and then they give all the passengers seat numbers. It's better to take an indirect flight.'

'What do you do at stops?'

'I pretend to be asleep. Usually they don't trouble me.'

'But this time you were found.'

'Only because of that man who was sitting next to me.' Mrs Quonsett said bitterly. 'I told him that it was a secret, but he told an air hostess. You can't trust anyone these days.'

'Mrs Quonsett,' Tanya said. 'I expect you heard what I said on the phone a few minutes ago. We're sending you back to Los Angeles tonight.'

'Yes, my dear, I thought you would. Just let me go and get a cup of tea first, and I'll be ready to go.'

'Oh no!' Tanya shook her head. 'You're not going anywhere alone.'

She asked a young agent called Peter Coakley to stay with Mrs Quonsett until her flight left.

'Don't let her get away from you for a second,' she told him. 'And be careful! She's full of little tricks.'

The old lady took Peter Coakley's arm. 'You're rather like my daughter's husband,' she said. 'He's a good-looking young man, too, but older than you of course. What nice people work for Trans America!' She looked at Tanya. '*Some* of them are nice, I mean,' she said.

Tanya felt sure that she had not seen the last of Mrs Ada Quonsett. Then she started to think about Mel Bakersfeld again, and wondered if he would come and see her.

Chapter 16   Mel's Argument with Vernon

Mel had decided that it would be impossible for him to leave the airport that night.

He was in his office, and had been getting the latest reports on what was happening on the airfield. Runway three zero was still blocked, and there were many delays. It was possible that the airport would have to be closed in a few hours.

Planes were still taking off over Meadowood, and many of the people who lived there had telephoned the airport to complain about the noise. Mel knew that there had also been a meeting, and now it seemed that some of the people from the meeting were coming to the airport. They would add greatly to the problems which he already had.

One good thing was that the emergency was over. The Air Force KC–135 had landed safely. But Mel still had the feeling that there was going to be another emergency, and that it would be worse than this one.

Cindy was waiting for him at the party. He must phone her immediately, although she wouldn't be very pleased to hear what he had to say.

He had to wait for several minutes before she came to the phone. He was surprised at how quiet her voice was. There was no anger in it now, only an icy calm.

He had not expected this, and found it difficult to talk to her. He told her that he would not be able to come to the party, and then paused, uncertain what to say next.

'Have you finished?' she asked coldly.

'Yes.'

'I'm not surprised at what you've just said. I never expected you to come. I knew that you were lying to me, as usual.'

'I wasn't lying, Cindy, and—'

'I thought you said you'd finished?'

Mel stopped. Why argue with her?

'You're staying at the airport?' she went on.

'I told you I was.'

'How long?'

'Until midnight. Possibly all night.'

'Then I'm coming to see you there.'

'Listen, Cindy, you can't come here. This is neither the time nor the place.'

46

'Then we'll make it the time. And for what I have to say, any place is good enough.'

He tried to reply, but she had already put down the telephone.

He sat in silence for a moment, and then, without knowing why, he called home. Mrs Sebastiani, who was looking after the children, answered.

'Is everything all right?' Mel asked. 'Are the girls in bed?'

'Roberta is, Mr Bakersfeld, but Libby's still awake.'

'May I speak to her?'

He heard her small feet running to the phone. As usual, she had a question for him: 'Daddy, does our blood keep going around and around for ever?'

'Not for ever, dear,' Mel told her. 'Nothing's for ever. Your blood has been going around for seven years so far.'

'I can feel my heart,' she said.

Mel was sure that she could. Libby had a good heart – whichever meaning you gave to the word.

He didn't know why he had telephoned home, but he was glad that he had. He supposed that Cindy would come to see him tonight. If she wanted to do something she usually did it. Perhaps she was right, and it was time to decide whether their hollow marriage should continue or not. If they talked about it here, at least the children would not have to hear them.

At the moment he had nothing to do. He left his office, and looked down over the crowded hall. He thought again that so much in the way airports worked was wrong and would have to change in the near future.

He saw a crowd in front of a notice that said 'Flight Two – Rome – the *Golden Argosy*'. Tanya was standing near it, talking to a group of passengers. Mel walked towards her, and when she saw him she left the passengers for a moment.

'I mustn't stop,' she said. 'I've got so much to do here. I thought you were going to a party!'

'My plans have changed,' Mel told her. 'Why are you still on duty?'

'I've been asked to stay. We're trying to make it possible for the *Golden Argosy* to take off on time. I think it's because Captain Demerest doesn't like waiting.'

'Don't think too badly of Captain Demerest,' Mel said, smiling. 'Although I do have doubts about him myself.'

Tanya pointed to a desk where two pretty girls were standing. 'That's the reason for your fight with Captain Demerest, isn't it?' she said. The two girls were busily writing insurance policies.

'Yes,' Mel admitted. 'That's a large part of the problem. Vernon thinks that we should stop selling flight insurance at airports. I don't. We had a battle about it in front of a lot of important people. I won, and Vernon hates being the loser.'

'I heard all about it.' Tanya looked hard at Mel. 'A lot of us agree with Captain Demerest.'

'I'll just have to disagree with a lot of you, then,' Mel replied.

He remembered his fight with Vernon well.

◆

It had happened at a meeting of the Airport Committee. Mel and all five committee members were present: a woman called Mrs Mildred Ackerman, two local businessmen, a union official and a teacher. The only outsider at the meeting was Captain Vernon Demerest. They decided to hear what he had to say first.

He spoke confidently and well. He argued that flight insurance was an insult to modern planes and pilots. Insurance policies were not sold at bus stations and garages! Why should they be sold at airports? Flying, he said, was a safe way to travel. Insurance companies and airports continued to sell flight insurance in order to make money out of the public. To sell huge insurance policies for a few dollars at airports was to invite criminals and madmen to murder for money, Vernon said.

'Do you have any facts to support this view?' Mrs Ackerman asked.

In reply, Vernon spoke of many cases of people who had blown up planes in an attempt to claim large amounts of money. They had failed, but others would continue to try.

Mrs Ackerman was not satisfied with this answer, and interrupted Vernon several times with questions. He was not used to being attacked, especially by a woman! People usually took orders from him. He lost his temper immediately, and made it clear that he thought her questions thoroughly stupid.

He had argued his case well, but nobody would agree with him because of his rude behaviour. Even before he began to speak, Mel knew that he had the advantage.

He told the meeting that many people, rightly or wrongly, were afraid of flying and liked to have insurance. If they couldn't buy it at the airport, they would simply buy it somewhere else. But his most important point was that the airport needed the money that it made by selling insurance policies. This was certain to be a popular argument with the committee.

After the meeting Vernon was waiting for him.

'Hello, Vernon,' Mel said quickly. 'I hope we're still friends.'

'We're not,' Vernon said, 'and we never have been.'

They both knew that this was true.

'You people who work on the ground, safe behind your little desks, can't possibly understand how we pilots feel about this matter. If you could only see things as clearly as I do—'

'I've been a pilot, too, Vernon,' Mel said. 'I wasn't always flying a desk, remember. And you may find this hard to believe, but you could be wrong. You're human too, I believe.'

'You're childish and stupid!' Vernon shouted. 'Keep away from me in future. I don't want to see you any more than I have to!'

If only it had never happened. Mel could not change his

opinion about insurance, but he wished that he had not made an enemy of Vernon.

◆

'You're dreaming,' he heard Tanya say. She was looking at him with a smile in her gentle, understanding eyes. Suddenly he knew that he wanted to get to know her better. He wished he could accept the offer she had made him earlier, of a good dinner at her apartment. But he had to accept the facts and behave responsibly. He couldn't leave the airport yet.

'Let's meet for dinner later tonight,' he said. 'Don't leave the airport without me.' He wanted to reach out and seize and hold her, but there were crowds of people all round them.

Tanya put her hand on his. 'I'll wait for you,' she said. 'I'll wait as long as you want me to.' Then she walked away through the crowd of waiting passengers.

Chapter 17   The *Golden Argosy*

Forty-five minutes before it was supposed to take off, the *Golden Argosy* was being prepared for its 5,000 mile flight to Rome. Some of the preparations for a long-distance flight take weeks, or even months. Others are made at the last moment.

The plane for Flight Two was a Boeing 707-320B. It had four engines and a speed of 620 miles an hour. It could carry 199 passengers.

Its last flight had been from Düsseldorf, Germany, to Lincoln International. During the flight, one of the engines had become too hot. The plane flew safely on three engines, and the passengers knew nothing about it. If necessary, it could have flown safely on one engine.

When it arrived at Lincoln International, a team of mechanics was waiting. The repairs took a long time and demanded great skill and care. The plane was not ready to fly again until two hours before it was to leave for Rome.

As soon as the repairs were finished, the job of loading the plane began. Large amounts of food and drink were taken on board, and so were newspapers and magazines. Finally, the passengers' luggage and bags of mail were loaded onto the plane. For some reason this was the most badly-managed part of the operation, and luggage was quite often lost or sent on the wrong flight.

Captain Harris had decided to ask for additional fuel tonight. The plane might be delayed for a long time on the runway before take-off, and the engines drank up fuel thirstily.

Anson Harris was not feeling very comfortable. After Vernon Demerest had told him to put on an airline shirt, he had borrowed one from a friend. It turned out to be too small for him. He decided to suffer in silence, as he did not intend to quarrel with Vernon. Harris was a professional pilot of the best kind, and he knew that it was dangerous to have quarrels with colleagues on a plane. With Vernon Demerest checking all his decisions tonight, he didn't want to make any mistakes.

Another man would be flying with Vernon Demerest and Anson Harris. He was the flight engineer, a thin young man called Cy Jordan, who was also a pilot.

A bus took them all to the Trans America wing of the airport. As well as the three men there were five air hostesses, one of them being Gwen Meighen. Captain Demerest greeted them with a bright 'Hi, girls!' Captain Harris, more formally, said 'Good evening.'

The bus moved slowly on the icy road. They could all feel the wind beating against it. When it stopped, they rushed towards the nearest door. They had their final preparations to make.

It was now that Captain Harris asked for additional fuel to be taken on board. Vernon checked the weather report. He learned that the weather would improve over the Atlantic, and that in Rome – and also in Naples – it would be fine.

The three men were ready for take-off when Gwen told them the news. 'The flight has been delayed by an hour,' she said. 'It seems that a lot of the passengers haven't arrived yet, because of the bad weather.'

'Oh no!' Vernon said angrily.

'Shall I bring you some coffee?' Gwen suggested.

'No, I'll go and get some in the terminal,' he said. 'Come with me, Gwen.'

As they were walking to the coffee shop, Vernon thought that the delay might turn out to be very useful for him. He could have another talk with Gwen, and this time they would discuss abortion.

Chapter 18   Guerrero Leaves Home

Nervously, D. O. Guerrero lit another cigarette from the end of his last one. His hands were shaking. He could not hide his fear – fear that the plane would leave without him, fear that he would be a failure once again.

He was on a bus on his way to the airport. The bus was moving very slowly through the snow and the heavy traffic. The passengers had been told that Flight Two, which they were all to travel on, had been delayed by an hour. But it might take them two or three hours to reach the airport, and Flight Two would not wait for them for ever.

There were only a few people on the bus. The driver said that he thought a lot of people had gone to the airport by car, to try to get there quickly. Everyone was talking about their chances of reaching the airport in time. Only Guerrero said nothing.

Most of the passengers were tourists, but there was also an Italian family with several children.

'Don't worry,' the driver said, 'we might just get there in time.' But they were still moving as slowly as before.

D. O. Guerrero passed his tongue over his dry lips. He needed ten or fifteen minutes at the airport, in order to buy his flight insurance. It would not be enough for him simply to catch the flight; he must have the insurance, too. He hadn't known that the weather would be so bad. He always had bad luck! All his great plans failed. But this one must not fail! He had already made one stupid mistake, he thought bitterly.

He was carrying no luggage except the small case that contained the bomb.

When he had gone to catch the airport bus, the ticket agent had asked him: 'Where are your cases, sir?'

Guerrero paused. 'I don't have anything but this.'

'No luggage for a trip to Rome, sir?'

The man looked surprised, and Guerrero thought that he was looking at him strangely.

'No,' he said, and hurried to the bus.

He knew that the agent would not forget his face. Later, when the questions were asked, he would remember the man with no luggage.

He should have brought some luggage!

But the plane would be completely destroyed, he reminded himself. They would not be able to prove anything against him. The flight insurance company would have to pay Inez.

Would this bus never get to the airport?

The Italians' children were running up and down the bus, and their baby was crying. Guerrero wanted to cry out at them to stop making that noise. Didn't they know that this was no time for playing or talking?

One of the running children fell into the seat next to

Guerrero and almost knocked his case onto the floor. He raised his hand to hit the child, and then, with an effort, managed to control himself. It would be stupid to draw attention to himself.

For a moment the boy looked into his eyes, and Guerrero found that he had to look away. They would all be dead soon. The children too. He couldn't afford to become soft-hearted now. In any case, it would all be over before they knew what was happening.

At last! The bus was moving faster. They might arrive in time. There seemed to be less traffic on the road now.

He was glad that he had not hit the child. But it was a pity that he had forgotten to bring any luggage with him. He began to worry about it. Perhaps the agent had telephoned the airport. The police might be waiting for him as he got off the bus.

If they were, Guerrero decided, he would pull the string and blow himself up. Whatever happened, he would not go to prison.

He wondered if Inez had found his note yet.

She had.

◆

Inez Guerrero came into the apartment, feeling very tired, and took off her wet coat. Her shoes were wet, too, and they hurt her feet. She was getting a cold, and her work in the coffee shop had seemed harder than usual today. She was not used to this kind of work, and now she ached with tiredness.

Two years ago, in her own comfortable home, Inez had been a pleasant-looking woman. Her pretty face had disappeared with their money. In better days, she had looked younger than she was; now she looked much older. She would have liked to take a hot bath, but there was only a cold, dirty bathroom which was shared by three families. Inez could not bear to go into it. Instead, she went into the living room. She had no idea where her husband

54

was. After a while she saw a note on the table. She read: "I won't be home for a few days. I'm going away. I expect to have some good news soon, which will surprise you. D. O."

Few things that her husband did surprised Inez. He had often made plans without asking her advice. Good news would be a wonderful surprise, but she didn't really believe that there would be any. She had seen her husband's plans fail so many times before.

But where was he going? And what money did he have? She knew that he had only a few dollars in his pocket, because they had counted their money the day before. They had had twenty-two dollars, and she had taken fourteen to help pay the rent. She remembered the look of sadness she had seen on her husband's face as he put the remaining few dollars into his pocket.

She decided to stop worrying and go to bed. She opened a drawer to put her clothes away and noticed that some things had been moved but that D. O. did not seem to have taken any clothes with him. In the drawer she found a piece of yellow paper; she learned from it that D. O. Guerrero had bought an airline ticket to Rome. He had paid forty-seven dollars, and had promised to pay the rest over two years.

Inez could not believe it. Why did he need an airline ticket? And why to Rome? How could he have paid forty-seven dollars?

Then she remembered her mother's ring. Before she looked in the box, she knew that it had gone. She was upset that he had sold the ring. It had been her last reminder of her past life, of her family, and of happier days.

Why had he gone to Rome?

Inez was not a very clever woman, but she understood her husband. Somehow she knew that he was in trouble, and that she must try to help him. He had been behaving strangely recently.

She did not think of leaving him to solve his own problems.

She had married him 'for better or worse', and the fact that it had been mainly 'worse' did not mean that her responsibility to him had lessened.

She forgot her tiredness, and hurried out in her wet clothes to find a telephone. She phoned Trans America and discovered that the flight to Rome had been delayed by an hour. It would leave at eleven o'clock instead of the usual ten o'clock.

It was now five past ten.

'Please, can you tell me if my husband is on the flight?' Inez asked. 'His name is D. O. Guerrero.'

'I'm sorry, but we are not allowed to give any information about passengers,' was the reply.

'But I'm his wife!' Inez cried.

'I'm sorry, but I can't break a company rule.'

She would have to go out to the airport herself, and try to find him.

She spent her last few dollars on a taxi. She was still on her way when the airport bus reached the terminal. D. O. Guerrero was the first person to step off it.

Chapter 19   Action at Meadowood

The Meadowood meeting was ending on a high note of excitement, just as lawyer Freemantle had planned that it should. The meeting was about to move on to the airport.

'I don't want to hear any excuses,' Elliott Freemantle said. 'Don't give me any stories about dinner being ready or the children being left alone. If your car is stuck in the snow, come with someone else. I'm going to the airport in order to help you people to get some justice.'

He paused, as a plane passed over with a noise like thunder.

'Good heavens! It's time someone did!'

Everyone laughed and cheered at this.

'I want all of you to come with me. Now I'll ask you just one question: Are you coming?'

'Yes!' they shouted. 'Yes!'

Elliott then told them that to take the airport to court was not enough. They also needed to have the attention and support of the public.

'How do we get that attention and support?' he asked, and then answered his own question: 'We get it by telling people all about our problem. We must interest the newspapers, radio and television, in any way that we can. We must give them a good story!'

The three reporters who were present smiled at this.

'Do as I tell you,' Elliott directed the people. 'Perhaps we'll cause a little trouble at the airport. I hear that they're rather busy tonight. But we must be careful not to break any laws.'

They were all ready to go. Elliott Freemantle looked at the papers that they had signed, and calculated that he had made about ten thousand dollars for himself from this evening's work. Not bad. The money was always the most important thing to him.

He did not know exactly what was going to happen at the airport, but he guessed that there would be plenty of action and excitement. He would keep these people satisfied and they would pay him well for this entertainment.

He noticed that one of the reporters was on the phone to his office. Good! Now it was time to leave for the airport.

Chapter 20   Joe Patroni Arrives

It had taken Patroni three hours to reach the airport. It usually took him 40 minutes.

When he came to the sign that said 'TWA Maintenance' he jumped out of his car, paused just long enough to light a cigar, and then got into the truck which was waiting for him. 'Get moving! As fast as you can!' he told the driver.

As they raced away, he called the control tower by radio telephone.

'We have a message for you,' he was told.

'What is it?'

'Joe,' the message went, 'I'll give you a box of cigars if you can get that plane off runway three zero tonight.' The message was from Mel Bakersfeld.

Patroni laughed. 'Now I've got something to work for!' he said.

Ingram told him what had been happening. First they had taken all the passengers off the plane and had tried to use its own power to move it. That had failed. Then all the luggage, mail and most of the plane's fuel had been taken off. Still they could not move it.

Patroni examined the ground around the plane. He did not seem to notice the cold or the snow that was falling on his hands and face. He found that the plane was badly stuck in the wet ground which lay under the ice and snow, but in spite of this he hoped that it would be possible to move it by its own power.

They would have to dig deep holes with sloping sides, and line them with wooden boards. Then, if they were lucky, the plane could be driven out. It was not going to be an easy job.

'The captain's still on board the plane,' Ingram told him. 'He refused to do what we asked him to when we first started trying to move the plane. Now I think he's a frightened man. He's made some bad mistakes tonight.'

'He sure has,' Patroni agreed. 'Get the men working, and I'll go and talk to him.'

Later, Patroni joined the maintenance men and worked with

them. He thought that the job would take at least an hour. It was now half past ten, and he hoped to be back home and in his warm bed soon after midnight.

Chapter 21 In the Coffee Shop

In the coffee shop Vernon Demerest ordered tea for Gwen and black coffee for himself. Coffee helped him to think clearly, and he would probably drink ten more cups on his way to Rome.

'We're both unusually quiet,' Gwen said in her gentle English voice. 'We hardly said a word on our way over here.' She turned her large eyes towards Vernon's face.

'I wasn't talking because I've been thinking,' he said.

'Thinking about what? About being a father?' Gwen said, smiling. 'Would you rather have a boy or a girl?'

'Oh Gwen, can't we be serious about this?'

'Why should you be worried if I'm not?' she asked. Then she took his hand and said: 'I'm sorry. I suppose it really is a bit of a shock — for both of us.'

This was the opportunity Vernon had been waiting for. 'We don't have to be parents if we don't want to be,' he said. Gwen took her hand away.

'I wondered how long it would take,' she said. 'You almost said it in the car, and then you decided to leave it until later, didn't you?'

'Leave what until later?'

'Oh really, Vernon! Why pretend? You want me to have an abortion, don't you? You've been thinking about it all the time, haven't you?'

'Yes,' he admitted.

'What's the matter? Did you think I'd never heard the word before?'

'I wasn't sure how you would feel about it.'

Gwen looked serious. 'I'm not sure how I feel.'

At least she hadn't said 'no' immediately.

'It would be the most sensible thing to do,' Vernon said. 'And it isn't dangerous at all.'

'I know. It's very simple, isn't it?'

Perhaps this was going to be easier than he had expected.

'Vernon,' she continued, 'have you really thought about this? You want to kill a human being, a person who is part of both of us, a person we have made with our love.'

'It is not a human being, Gwen,' he said firmly. 'It would be later, but it isn't now.'

'Do you mean that you wouldn't kill it later, but you would now?'

'Don't twist my words around, Gwen.'

'I suppose you think I'm being stupid,' she said sadly, 'but I do love you, Vernon, I really do.'

'I know,' he said. 'That's why this is so difficult for both of us.'

Gwen sighed. 'I suppose in the end I'll be sensible. I'll have an abortion. But I must have a little time to think about it first.'

'Of course. But we must act as quickly as possible.'

'I promise you I'll decide before the end of this trip.'

As they got up to leave the coffee shop, Gwen said: 'I'm really lucky to have you, Vernon. Some men would have walked away and left me.'

'I won't leave you.'

But he would leave her. He had just decided to. When the trip to Naples and the abortion were over, he would end the affair as delicately as he could. Gwen knew how to behave, and would not make any difficulties for him. Even if she did make trouble, he could handle the situation. He had ended love affairs before now.

It was true that he cared deeply for Gwen. It would not be easy to leave her, but it was time to finish the affair. He did not intend to leave Sarah or to make any great changes to his lifestyle.

He touched Gwen's arm. 'You go on. I'll follow in a minute.'

He had just seen Mel Bakersfeld and, what was worse, he knew that Mel had seen him.

Mel was talking to Ned Ordway, the man who was chief of police at the airport.

'I've just heard that we're to have visitors later,' Ordway told him.

'We have several thousand already.'

'I don't mean passengers. I mean the people from Meadowood. They've just had a meeting, and now they're coming to see you.'

'Oh no!' Mel said. 'I'm busy enough tonight without them.'

'I can't keep them out unless they break the law,' Ordway said. 'I've told my men what's going to happen, and they'll handle it carefully. We don't want any violence here.'

Mel had complete confidence in Ned Ordway. He knew he was a good policeman.

'Any other trouble tonight?' he asked.

'More fights than usual. It's because of all the flight delays. All the bars are full.' He added: 'I'll let you know when the Meadowood crowd get here.'

As Ordway walked away, Mel saw Vernon coming towards him. 'Good evening, Vernon,' he said.

'Hi.'

'I hear you know all there is to know about snow clearing now.'

'I don't need to know much to see that a bad job is being done.'

'Do you know how much snow there has been?' Mel asked.

'I know better than you, I expect. Part of my job is to read weather reports.'

'We've had about 30 centimetres of snow in the last 24 hours.'

'Then clear it!'

It was useless to try to discuss this matter with Vernon. Mel knew that his critical report on snow clearing had been written for reasons of personal dislike.

'I'll think of you here, stuck in the snow, when I'm enjoying the sun in Naples,' Vernon said, and walked off laughing.

But he soon stopped laughing when he saw the two girls selling insurance policies. They reminded him of a fight that Mel Bakersfeld had won. He wondered if any Flight Two passengers were buying insurance. He would like to tell them not to waste their money!

As he watched, a thin, nervous-looking man joined the line of people waiting at the desk. He kept looking at the clock, and seemed to be worried because there were so many people in front of him. He should have arrived earlier if he wanted to stand in line for flight insurance, Vernon thought.

As he hurried away, he heard the announcement: 'Trans America Airlines announce the departure of Flight Two, the *Golden Argosy*, for Rome–'

Chapter 22   Guerrero Insures Himself

The flight departure announcement meant something different to each person who heard it.

To some it meant a business trip, to others a holiday and the possibility of adventure. To some it meant the sadness of parting, and to others a happy meeting. Some heard the announcement with fear, and others with joy. They were all about to leave the safety of the ground for the adventure of the skies.

More than a hundred and fifty Flight Two passengers heard the announcement, and hurried to Gate 47.

Gwen Meighen welcomed them on board the plane. For her, the other girls and the three men in the team, this was the beginning of many hours of hard work.

Mel Bakersfeld heard the announcement, and remembered that the *Golden Argosy* was Vernon's flight. He wished that he and Vernon could find some way of being polite to each other. Perhaps they couldn't be friends, but he didn't want them to be enemies for the rest of their lives. Part of the trouble was that Vernon, like many pilots, was terribly proud.

Mel wished that he was still able to fly a plane. He had enjoyed being a pilot, but now he could only fly as a passenger. He was jealous of the people who were flying off into the Italian sunshine. He needed a little sunshine in his life, too.

◆

Ned Ordway heard the announcement as he sat in his small office. He had just received a message from a police car, telling him that the Meadowood people had arrived at the airport.

◆

Mrs Ada Quonsett stopped talking for a moment, and listened to the flight announcement. She was sitting next to Peter Coakley, and telling him all about her dead husband.

'Such a dear person,' she sighed. 'So wise and good-looking. When he was young he looked rather like you.'

Peter Coakley was tired of hearing about Herbert Quonsett. He felt such a fool, sitting here in his uniform looking after this old grandmother. It was bad luck that her flight to Los Angeles had been delayed by the storm. He hoped that it would be able to take off soon.

63

He had already forgotten Tanya's warning: 'Be careful. She's full of little tricks.' He didn't realize that making him tired of her could be part of the old lady's plan.

'Rome!' Mrs Quonsett cried. 'Imagine that! It must be so interesting to work in an airport, especially for an intelligent young man like you. My dear husband always wanted us to visit Rome, but we never did.'

While she was talking, she was also thinking. Why not go to Rome? That would be a story to tell her daughter! Her greatest success of all! She knew that she could easily escape from this child in a man's uniform. Gate 47, wasn't it? Yes, she would try.

Suddenly she made a low noise and put her hand to her mouth. 'Oh dear! Oh dear!' she cried weakly.

Peter Coakley looked frightened.

'What is it, Mrs Quonsett? What's wrong?'

She closed her eyes, breathing noisily.

'I'm so sorry. I'm afraid I don't feel at all well.'

'Do you want me to get you a doctor?'

'I don't want to be any trouble!'

'You won't be.'

'No.' Mrs Quonsett shook her head weakly. 'I think I'll just go to the ladies' room. I expect I'll be all right.'

The young agent looked doubtful.

'Are you sure?'

'Yes, quite sure.'

She took his arm. At the door of the ladies' room she turned to him and said: 'You're so kind to an old lady. Thank you so much. You won't go away, will you?'

'No, of course not.'

In the ladies' room she looked for a woman with a kind face. She soon found one.

'Excuse me,' she said. 'I'm not feeling very well. Could you help me?'

'Of course. Would you like—?'

'No — please. I just want to send a message. There's a young man in a Trans America uniform waiting outside the door. His name is Peter Coakley. Please tell him that, yes, I *would* like him to send for a doctor.'

When he had gone to fetch a doctor, she sent the woman off to tell her daughter what had happened. Her daughter, she said, was "a lady in a long blue coat, with a little white dog". She hoped that the woman wouldn't waste too much time looking for her! She was feeling quite proud of her powers of imagination.

When the kind woman had gone, Ada Quonsett came out of the ladies' room and walked quickly towards Gate 47.

Tanya Livingston was dealing with a passenger who said that his luggage had been damaged, and demanded that the airport should buy him a new case. Tanya didn't believe that the case had been damaged at the airport. It looked very old. Some people will always try to cheat, she thought.

She decided that when she had finished with this man, she would go to Gate 47. Perhaps she would be needed there.

◆

D. O. Guerrero heard the flight departure announcement while in the line of people waiting in front of the insurance desk. It was Guerrero, appearing hurried and nervous, whom Vernon Demerest had seen arrive there.

There were still four people in front of him. He would miss the flight. But he must not! He could not!

He was shaking with nerves. He looked at the clock again. He had to do something! He could not just stand still and see his plan fail!

He pushed his way to the front of the line. 'Please — my flight has been called — the one to Rome. I need insurance! I can't wait!'

'We're all waiting,' a man said. 'Get here earlier next time.'
Guerrero wanted to say: 'There won't be a next time,' but instead
he looked at the girl and said: 'Please!' again.

To his surprise she smiled and asked: 'Did you say you were
going to Rome?'

'Yes, yes. The flight's been called.'

'I know. The *Golden Argosy*.'

She smiled at all the people who were waiting.

'This gentleman seems to be in a hurry. I'm sure you'll excuse
me if I see to him first.'

◆

The girl was called Bunnie Vorobioff. She was a great success at
selling insurance.

When she smiled at the people who had been waiting before
D. O. Guerrero, nobody complained. Even Guerrero, who did
not usually take much notice of women, thought that she was
attractive. She had a wide, white smile and a wonderful figure.

Bunnie knew exactly how much power she had over men. She
was using that power for a special reason today. D. O. Guerrero
could not know this, but the insurance company that Bunnie
worked for was holding a competition, with a big prize for the
girl who could sell the largest amount of insurance. Guerrero was
going to Rome. Bunnie hoped that she would be able to sell him
a large policy for such a long flight.

'What kind of policy do you wish to buy?' she asked him.

'Life – seventy-five thousand dollars.'

This policy would cost him two and a half dollars.

He could hardly speak, and when he tried to light a cigarette
his hand shook violently. He felt sure that everyone was looking
at him and wondering why he wanted such a huge policy.

'But that is a small policy!' Bunnie cried. She leaned forward
and smiled invitingly at him.

'Small? – I thought it was the biggest.'

'Oh no!' Bunnie laughed. 'Why not take a three hundred thousand dollar policy? Most people do. It only costs ten dollars.'

He had not known that! It would be a fortune for Inez.

'Yes,' he said eagerly. 'Please – yes.'

Then he remembered something. Did he have ten dollars left in the world?

He began to search feverishly through his pockets. He found four dollars. Behind him the other people were beginning to complain again.

'You can give me Italian money,' Bunnie said.

'I don't have any.' He realized immediately that this was another mistake. Now he had told one person that he had no luggage, and another that he had no money. But the plane will be completely destroyed, he reminded himself. No proof will remain.

To his surprise he found five dollars in a pocket. Then he found a few coins. Yes! He had enough! He could not hide his excitement.

But now it was Bunnie's turn to stop. She had been watching his face while he counted his money, and in it she had seen hopelessness. Should she refuse to sell this man a policy?

Bunnie wanted to win the prize. She paused for only a few seconds before she insured D. O. Guerrero's life for three hundred thousand dollars. He posted the policy to his wife, Inez. Then he rushed towards Gate 47 and Flight Two.

Chapter 23   Mrs Quonsett Escapes

Customs Officer Harry Standish did not hear the flight departure announcement, but he knew that it had been made. He had a special interest in Flight Two, because Judy would be travelling on it. Judy was a fine young girl, and a great favourite with her uncle Harry.

He was a very busy man, but he found time to walk over to Gate 47 to say goodbye to her. When she had gone he stood near the gate for a while, watching the last few passengers hurry by. Tanya Livingston was watching them, too.

A tall, fair young man went through the gate. He seemed to be the last one. Tanya left as soon as he had disappeared, but Standish saw two other people arrive. One of them was a small figure in black, a little old lady.

'My son just went through this gate,' he heard her say to a ticket agent. 'He's a tall, fair young man. He's forgotten all his money. May I take it to him, please?'

The agent was busy with his papers. 'Go and ask an air hostess,' he said, smiling kindly at the old lady.

The last passenger came a moment later. He was a thin man who was carrying a small case. Something about this man attracted the officer's attention. He knew immediately, from his long experience in dealing with the public, that there was something strange about him.

◆

He had successfully bought and posted the insurance policy, and he was on the plane. D. O. Guerrero felt full of confidence. All his difficulties were over.

'Have a pleasant flight, sir,' the agent at the gate had said to him.

His seat was by the window. There was an empty seat in the centre, and then another man. He closed his eyes. He felt happier than he had for a long time. He put his fingers inside the case and felt the important piece of string. When he pulled it, the plane would be destroyed immediately.

Immediately? He hoped that there would be a last second in

which he would know about his success. And then – thank heavens – no more.

He opened his eyes. One of the air hostesses was counting the passengers.

During the count, Mrs Ada Quonsett was hiding in one of the toilets. If she could remain hidden now, she knew that she had a good chance of reaching Rome. It had been a nasty shock seeing that red-haired woman at the gate, but in the end all her plans had gone well.

She opened the door a little, and looked out. There was an empty seat between two men, and she decided to slip into it. As she did so, she was included in the passenger count.

She hoped that she would find someone interesting to talk to during the flight. She knew that sooner or later she would be found and sent back to Los Angeles, but before that happened she intended to enjoy a film, a good meal and some pleasant conversation.

She looked at the man on her left. He had a thin, yellowish face, and looked as if he needed a good dinner. Perhaps he was worried about something. He had a small case on his knees, and he was holding it firmly. Mrs Quonsett always wanted to know about other people, and she wondered what was inside the case.

◆

Standish was talking to Tanya.

'I watched the last passengers get on Flight Two,' he told her. 'There was one man I felt very worried about. If he'd been arriving instead of leaving, I would have asked him to open his case.'

'What do you think he's doing?'

'I don't know. Oh, perhaps I'm wrong, but I have a strange feeling about him.'

As Tanya walked back to her office, she wondered what – if

anything – she should do about this.

She found Peter Coakley waiting for her there.

'What are you doing here?'

He had to tell her that the little old lady had been too clever for him.

Tanya was extremely angry. 'Didn't I warn you about her?' she shouted.

All they could do now was telephone the gates and warn all the agents not to allow an old lady in black to get on a plane.

Tanya knew that it was total war between Mrs Quonsett and her – and the old lady was winning.

For a moment, her conversation with Standish was forgotten.

◆

At the controls of the *Golden Argosy*, Vernon Demerest was beginning to lose his temper.

'What are we waiting for? Why can't we take off?'

He saw Gwen coming towards him. 'Gwen! What's happening?'

She looked worried. 'The passenger count keeps going wrong. We're checking it now. We seem to have one passenger too many.'

That, Vernon thought, was not a good enough reason to delay their take-off any longer, especially on a night like this, when traffic was very heavy. A delay like this was expensive as well as annoying.

He did not waste time, but found the officer who was responsible for checking the passengers' tickets.

'Look,' he said, 'the engines are running. We're using up fuel fast. There's a runway ready for us now, but there may not be later. If we wait for you to fool around any longer, there may be a really big delay. Now decide what you are going to do – but please, make the right decision!'

As usual, Vernon won. The passengers were not checked again.

'Rome – and Naples – here we come!'

It was 11 o'clock. A tired, badly dressed woman almost fell as she ran towards Gate 47. She had no breath left to ask questions, but she could see that it was unnecessary to ask.

Inez Guerrero saw the lights of a plane moving away from her into the darkness. She had arrived too late.

Chapter 24   Take-Off

The minutes just before take-off were a busy time for Gwen Meighen. First she had to welcome the passengers on board the plane. With her pleasant voice she tried to make the insincere words mean something. Then there were more important announcements to make, telling the passengers what to do in an emergency.

They had not yet reached the runway when Gwen finished these. She noticed that they seemed to be moving slowly tonight, and guessed that this was because of the snow and the heavy traffic. She could hear the wind blowing hard outside.

Her last announcement was the one she enjoyed making least. She had to tell the passengers that just after take-off the power of the engines would be reduced in order to lessen the noise they made. She told them that this always happened. It did not, as she knew. It was a dangerous thing to do, but Lincoln International had decided that planes which took off over Meadowood must do it.

She knew what Vernon thought about this rule. He called it stupid and extremely dangerous. Thinking of him, she smiled. There were so many things about him that she loved.

Looking out of the window, she could see the lights of another plane in front of them, and others waiting behind them.

She sat down and prepared herself for the take-off. As the noise of the engines grew, there was only one question in her mind: Vernon's child and her own — should it live or die? How could anyone expect her to decide such a thing?

Although Gwen had told the passengers that power would be reduced after take-off to lessen the noise, Captain Harris had decided that it would be too dangerous to do this during the storm. The people of Meadowood might complain, but he would not risk his plane and the lives of his passengers. At least this was one thing that he and Vernon Demerest agreed about!

They had been lucky to reach the runway so quickly. The additional fuel taken on by Harris had not been needed. Now they were at the front of a long line of waiting planes, at the beginning of runway two five.

Two five was cut across by another runway, one seven, left. As he waited, Harris could see through the snow the lights of a plane about to land on one seven, left. It crossed their path, and immediately he heard the controller's voice say: 'Trans America Two cleared for take-off. Go now!'

He did not wait for a second. Above the airfield another plane was already approaching one seven, left.

The *Golden Argosy* burst forward along the runway and then up into the clouds. The beginning of the flight would be rough, but soon they would be up in the clear sky, flying above the storm.

Although Keith Bakersfeld was not controlling the take-off of Flight Two, he heard and recognized Vernon Demerest's voice. Like Mel, Keith was not particularly friendly with his sister's husband, although he had never quarrelled with him.

As he worked, he kept putting his hand into his pocket to touch the key to the hotel room that he had taken.

His thoughts of death were interrupted by Wayne Tevis.

'Stop work for a few minutes,' he told Keith. 'Your brother is here to see you.'

'Hello,' Mel said. 'How are things?'

'All right, I suppose.'

Mel had brought two cups of coffee with him. He was always thoughtful like that. Keith watched his own hand shake as he took the cup. Mel was shocked by his appearance. He had never seen his brother looking so tired and ill before.

Their father had been one of the first pilots. He had loved flying, and had been killed performing a daring trick in an air show. He had pushed his sons into a life in aviation, and perhaps, Mel thought, it had been the wrong thing to do to Keith.

He opened the door. 'Come out for a moment, Keith. We'll be able to talk more easily out here.'

When they were outside the door, he continued quietly. 'You look ill, Keith, as I'm sure you know. Please be honest with me, and tell me what's wrong. You look as if you need a holiday – or perhaps more than a holiday – from Air Traffic Control.'

Keith smiled at him for the first time. 'You've been talking to Natalie.'

This was true. Mel wondered if Keith knew how lucky he had been in his choice of a wife. He had always been a little jealous of their relationship. He couldn't help feeling that Natalie was a better woman than Cindy.

'Keith,' he said, 'is it something to do with the accident at Leesburg? Is there something that you know about that crash that nobody else knows? Is that what's worrying you?'

Keith paused for a moment before he answered, 'Yes.'

'Please tell me, Keith. Let me try to help you.'

'No. I can't.'

But why not? he thought. He was going to kill himself. Perhaps he should share his terrible secret with his brother before he died. They had always been very close to one another.

'You know something about the accident,' he began slowly,

73

'but you don't know everything.'

'Go on. I'm listening.'

The words began to pour out in a flood. Suddenly Keith wanted very much to tell Mel that the accident had been completely his fault. He, and only he, had killed the Redfern family and ruined the lives of Perry Yount and George Wallace.

Without warning, a door opened. 'Oh Mr Bakersfeld,' a voice said. 'Could you phone Ned Ordway? He's been looking everywhere for you. So has Danny Farrow.'

Mel wanted to cry out, to shout for silence, or at least a delay. But it was too late. Keith had stopped talking immediately. He was alone again, and as lonely as before. He was sorry now that he had started to tell Mel his secret. It was better that it should die with him.

He went back to the radar room, and Mel knew that he would hear no more from him tonight. Mel himself had to talk to Danny Farrow and Ned Ordway. The police chief wanted to tell him that the Meadowood people were beginning to arrive at the airport. So far they had caused no trouble. But there was something else.

A policeman had found a woman wandering about the airport crying. She was unable to tell him what was wrong with her, and he hadn't wanted to frighten her by taking her to the police station.

'Then what did you do with her?' Mel asked.

'I left her sitting outside your office. It's quiet there, and she can calm down and collect her thoughts.'

'Is she alone?'

'One of my men was with her, but he may have left by now. I'm sure she isn't dangerous.'

'I'm going back to my office in a few minutes,' Mel said. 'I'll speak to her then.' He hoped that he would have more success in helping this woman than he had had with his brother. He was still very worried about Keith.

'Did you take her name?'

'Yes, I've got it here. Guerrero. Mrs Inez Guerrero.'

◆

Tanya Livingston cried, 'You mean Mrs Quonsett's on board Flight Two?'

'I'm afraid so, Mrs Livingston,' the ticket agent said.

He was in Tanya's office. So was an extremely red-faced Peter Coakley.

'I didn't think she could get past me like that,' the agent went on. 'But, I was so busy that she did. I was doing the work of two people all evening.'

'Yes, I know,' Tanya said. She couldn't blame him. In fact, she blamed herself.

'She said that her son had forgotten his money, and that she wanted to go and give it to him.'

'She often says that. It's one of her many tricks.'

'She sure can fool you,' poor Peter Coakley said.

There was no doubt about it. Ada Quonsett was on her way to Rome. The flight had already taken off, and there were no stops. The old lady had won her battle against Tanya.

When Peter Coakley and the agent had left, Bert Weatherby, the Transport Manager, wanted to see Tanya. She had to take full responsibility for Mrs Quonsett's presence on Flight Two.

'Send a radio message to the captain and tell him what has happened,' Weatherby told Tanya. 'By the way, who is the captain?'

'Captain Demerest.'

'Oh no! He always loves it when other people make mistakes! Well, it was your mistake, and you must deal with it.'

'Yes, sir.'

Tanya tried to tell him about her conversation with Standish, but Weatherby had heard enough already.

'Forget it!' he shouted. 'Let Italian Customs deal with the man. It isn't our problem.'

But Tanya couldn't help worrying about the thin man with the small case.

Chapter 25   Cindy's Decision

In a taxi on her way to the airport, Cindy Bakersfeld leaned back and closed her eyes. She had a lot to think about.

Her marriage to Mel was over. They had been growing slowly apart for a long time, and now Cindy realized that they had reached the end. Early in their marriage they had had the wonderful social life that she wanted, but now Mel seemed to have only one interest in life – the airport.

The trouble had really begun at the time when Mel met President Kennedy. Cindy had hoped for invitations to the White House, and had dreamed of calling Jackie Kennedy her friend. It had never happened. After President Kennedy's death Mel put everything into his job. That left Cindy with nothing. She knew that she was not a very clever woman, and now her chief aim in life was for her daughters to become great social successes.

This was something that Lionel would be able to help her with. As Mel had guessed, Cindy had found a lover. Lionel came from an old and respected family, and had plenty of money. He had left his wife, and now he wanted to marry Cindy. He was ready to act as a father to Roberta and Libby.

True, he was not young or attractive, as Mel had been when she married him, but Cindy could see that there would be a lot of advantages in being married to such a man.

She did not like making decisions, and she could not help remembering that she had once been happy with Mel, but she knew that the time for action had come. They could not go on living together.

She paid the taxi-driver and hurried to Mel's office. There was a badly dressed middle-aged woman in wet clothes waiting outside the office. Her eyes were red from crying. Cindy did not take much notice of her, but went into the office and sat down to wait for Mel.

When he came in a few minutes later, he seemed surprised to see her there. He had not really expected her to come, and wondered exactly what she wanted. She looked very beautiful tonight. He noticed it, but it no longer seemed to touch him.

'Why have you come here?' he asked.

'Why do you think?'

'I think you want a fight. Don't we fight enough at home, without starting here?'

'You don't spend much time at home these days.'

'I would if it was more pleasant there.'

It seemed that they could not talk to each other for a few minutes without quarrelling.

'You pretend to be so busy here,' she continued.

'Tonight I am.'

'Tonight! What about all the other times?'

'I admit it,' Mel said. 'Sometimes it has been more pleasant to stay here than to come home to a fight with you.'

'You're being honest about it for the first time!'

'And when I *do* come home,' he went on, 'you always seem to want to go out to some stupid party.'

'Stupid party!' Cindy shouted angrily. 'So you never intended to come to the party tonight. I knew you wouldn't come! You're nothing but a liar!'

'Calm down, Cindy.'

'I won't calm down!'

What had happened to them? Mel wondered. Why were they

behaving like two children?

'I'm not a liar,' he said, 'although I am sometimes glad that my work here keeps me away from home. I really am busy tonight. For a start, I must see that woman who's waiting outside the door. She's in trouble.'

'Your wife's in trouble,' Cindy said. 'That woman can wait.'

'All right.'

'Mel,' she went on, 'this is the end for us, isn't it?'

He did not want to agree with her, but he had to face the truth. 'Yes, I'm afraid it is. Neither of us will ever change enough to please the other.'

'I've been thinking about this,' Cindy said slowly, 'and I think I want a divorce.'

'Are you sure? It's a big step to take.'

'Yes, I'm sure.'

'So am I,' Mel said sadly. 'I think it's the right decision for us to make.'

There was no anger now. They were both very calm.

'I'm sorry,' Cindy said,

'I'm sorry, too.' Mel was close to tears at the thought of losing his daughters. They would remain with their mother. He knew that he would miss his talks with Libby very badly. Earlier this evening she had asked him for a 'map of February'. Well, now he had one.

There was a knock at the door.

'I'm sorry to interrupt,' Ordway said.

'That's all right. What is it?'

'The Meadowood people are here to see you.'

He brought six representatives of Meadowood into the office. They were followed by Elliott Freemantle and three reporters. Cindy remained where she was, silent and angry at the interruption.

Through the open door, Mel saw that the woman who had

been waiting was standing now. When he looked again a moment later, he noticed that she had gone.

Chapter 26   Mrs Quonsett Enjoys Herself

Trans America Flight Two was twenty minutes out of Lincoln International, and on course for Rome. It was flying above the storm, in a clear sky.

Inside the plane, a radio message was being received. Anson Harris, Cy Jordan and Vernon all laughed as they listened to the description of Mrs Ada Quonsett, the stowaway.

'I don't believe it!' Jordan said.

'I do!' Vernon laughed. 'It's so easy to get past those fools on the ground. Even an old grandmother is too clever for them!'

He asked Gwen to go and look for the old lady. When she came back she was laughing, too. 'She's all in black, and about eighty years old. A real threat to public safety! Shall I ask her to show me her ticket?'

'No,' Vernon said, 'don't do that.'

The others looked at him in surprise.

'Let her enjoy the flight. Give her a nice dinner and let her see the film. You can tell her that we know who she is just before we get to Rome.'

'Well, Vernon, you can be quite likeable sometimes!' Gwen said.

'I didn't know you liked old ladies, Vernon,' Harris said, when Gwen had gone.

Vernon laughed. 'I prefer young ones. I'm not like you, Anson!'

Everyone knew that Harris had never cheated on his wife. When he was away from home on flights, Vernon had seen him reading books or going to a film – alone.

'How many children have you got?' he asked.

'Seven. Four we intended to have, and three we didn't. But we're glad to have them all.'

'The ones you didn't intend to have. Did you ever consider doing anything about them? Before they were born?'

'Do you mean abortion?' Harris asked sharply.

'Yes.'

'Never. It's something I have very strong views about.'

'Because of your religion?'

'No. I'm not a very religious man.'

'Why then?'

'Do you really want to hear all about it?'

'Why not? We have all night.'

They would be able to hear any radio calls that might come in, and they were free to talk.

Harris told Vernon what he believed. He said that society had progressed by caring about people and by respecting their rights. Abortion refused a child the right to life, and to him this was as bad as murder.

This was not at all what Vernon wanted to hear.

'You should have been a lawyer, not a pilot,' he told Harris.

'I told you that I had strong feelings about this. You don't need to be religious to respect human life.'

'Or to have a lot of stupid ideas! Anyway, abortion is becoming easier all the time. Not many people agree with you.'

'Then our society is taking a step backwards.' Harris replied firmly.

'So you think it's right for unwanted children to grow up without any of the advantages of normal family life, do you?'

'No, of course not. We should help them by trying to improve our society, not by killing them.'

Vernon was beginning to wish that he had never started this conversation.

'Let's get some food before the passengers eat it all,' he said. He didn't want to listen to any more of Harris and his old woman's arguments. Of course it would be right for Gwen to have an abortion – as soon as possible!

Mrs Quonsett was enjoying a pleasant conversation with one of her neighbours, who was a musician.

'How wonderful,' she said. 'My husband loved good music. He played a little himself, but not professionally, of course. What a pity he can't be here to talk to you!'

Her new friend had already bought her one drink, and now he asked her if she would like another.

'How kind of you,' she said. 'Perhaps I shouldn't say yes, but I really think I will.'

Her other neighbour was rather a disappointment. She had tried to talk to him, but he had said almost nothing. He just sat there with his case on his knees.

'Poor man,' she said to herself. 'Perhaps he has problems.'

She enjoyed her second drink even more than the first one. Soon she would be having dinner, and then there would be a film. She had never felt happier in her life.

Guerrero calculated that they were flying over the Detroit area. He was correct. There had been several useful announcements about the position and speed of the plane and, like every other passenger, he had a flight map. In about two and a half hours they would be flying over the coast of Newfoundland, and an hour after that would be the best time to pull the string and blow them all up.

Now that the time was near, he wanted it to come quickly. He did not want to talk to anybody, especially not to that annoying old woman in the next seat. He just wanted to close his eyes and dream about all the money that would be coming to Inez and the children.

He wondered if they would ever guess what he had done for

them, and thank him for it. But there was one strange thing – he couldn't remember their faces any more. It was easier for him to imagine the money.

Then he must have fallen asleep. When he woke up, a voice was saying: 'Are you ready for your dinner, sir? May I take your case?'

Chapter 27 Mel Meets Elliott Freemantle

As soon as Mel met Elliott Freemantle, the lawyer, he disliked him. Ten minutes later, he knew that he hated the man.

It seemed that Freemantle was being as unpleasant as possible. He replied rudely to everything that Mel said. Mel soon realized that the lawyer was trying to make him lose his temper. He continued to speak calmly and politely to him, but he was finding it increasingly difficult.

Freemantle claimed that he did not care that people's lives were being ruined by the noise from the airport.

'We do care,' Mel told him. 'We know that there's a problem, and we're doing our best to solve it.'

'Then your best is not good enough. And what have you done? You've just made a lot of empty promises, that's all.'

'That's not true. We only use runway two five – which is the runway nearest to Meadowood – when we have to. The airport loses money by doing this. Perhaps you don't know this, but we've had many meetings with representatives of Meadowood before.'

'Perhaps you didn't tell them the truth at all those other meetings. This meeting is going to be very different!'

Mel decided not to answer. He saw that the reporters were writing busily, and knew that this was what Freemantle wanted. He felt sorry for Cindy, who had no interest at all in this matter.

'You tell us that the runway nearest to Meadowood is not used,' Elliot continued, 'but it was certainly in use tonight.'

'There's been a storm,' Mel said. 'I suppose that you've all noticed it? We had to use two five because three zero is blocked.'

'We understand the reason, Mr Bakersfeld,' an older man said, 'but that doesn't help us. We still suffer from the noise. My name is Floyd Zanetta, and–'

'Excuse me,' Elliott Freemantle interrupted. 'There's another point that I should like to make. We ought to tell you that we intend to take this airport to court, and we intend to win our case. Your airport, Mr Bakersfeld, is going to be closed down.'

Of course Elliott knew that this would never happen. He was speaking well tonight, though. He wished that he could be heard by a larger group of people.

'You are free to try anything you like,' Mel said, 'but I don't believe that any court would close down this airport.'

'Oh? I didn't know that you were a lawyer!'

'I'm not, as I'm sure you know.'

'Well, I am a lawyer, you see,' Elliott Freemantle said, 'and I can tell you that there have been many cases like this. The airports have lost them.'

He named several cases. Mel felt rather amused. He knew all about them, and understood that the situations had been very different from this one. There were many other cases which the airports had won, but of course Elliott did not mention them.

Mel decided that the lawyer had said enough, and that it was time for him to speak. 'Since we are all here, there are some things I would like to say to you on the subject of airports and noise generally,' he said.

'That won't be necessary.'

'Really, Mr Freemantle? I've listened to everything you've had to say. Don't you think you ought to listen to me now? I'm sure the press will be interested in this.'

'I think we ought–' Zanetta started to say.

'Let Mr Freemantle answer me,' Mel said sharply.

'There's no need to shout or to be rude,' Elliott said, smiling.

'Oh? Then why have you been doing both those things yourself?'

'Are you losing your temper, Mr Bakersfeld?'

'No,' Mel said. 'I know that you would like me to, but I'm not going to. I'm going to tell you all the facts about this situation.'

He told them how difficult it was to reduce the noise that a huge plane makes when it takes off and lands. Planes were getting bigger and noisier all the time, too. There was no easy answer to the Meadowood problem. In the end, the people would probably have to move from there. The airport would pay them for the loss of their homes.

'Yes! You will pay them!' Elliott Freemantle said, rising to his feet, 'and sooner than you think. We'll see you in court.' He went out, and the others followed him quietly.

'I'm sorry about that,' Mel told Cindy.

'You should have married the airport, not me.'

One of the reporters, a young man called Tomlinson, came back into the office.

'Mr Bakersfeld, could I see you for a moment?'

'What is it?' Mel asked. He felt terribly tired.

'I thought you'd like to see this.'

It was one of the papers that Elliott Freemantle had given to the people at the meeting to sign, in order to name him as their lawyer. Mel looked at Tomlinson.

'How many people signed this?'

'I'm not sure. Several hundred, I think.'

Now Mel understood what Freemantle was trying to do.

'Will you mention this in your story?'

'Yes, but I don't know whether or not my paper will print it.'

84

'Thanks for telling me about it.' He wished that he had known about the money earlier.

'I'd like to talk to you about the airport, if you have time,' the reporter said.

'Certainly,' Mel replied, 'but not just now. At the moment there are lots of problems all demanding my attention. I hope we'll have a chance to talk later tonight.'

Chapter 28   The Search for Inez

As Tomlinson left Mel's office, Cindy stood up.

'You have lots of problems demanding your attention,' she said bitterly, 'and I'm sure they're all more important to you than your wife.'

'Cindy, I really do have to work.'

'Yes, but you love it, don't you? You love your work much more than you love me or the children or a good social life.'

'Why are we fighting? We don't have to fight any more.'

'No,' Cindy said. 'I suppose not.'

There was a silence.

'Are you quite sure about the divorce?' Mel asked. 'If you have any doubts—'

'I haven't, and neither have you really.'

'That's true.'

She almost started to tell him about Lionel, but then decided that it would be better to keep it a secret.

There was a light knock at the door.

'Again!' Cindy exclaimed.

Tanya Livingston came in. 'Mel, I need some advice—' she began. Then she saw Cindy, and stopped. 'Excuse me. I thought you were alone.'

'He will be very soon,' Cindy said, looking hard at Tanya.

Tanya went red. 'I'm sorry, Mrs Bakersfeld. I didn't mean to interrupt you.'

'I'm sure that it's time we were interrupted,' Cindy went on, looking at Mel. 'After all, it must be at least two minutes since someone came in.' She turned to Tanya. 'How do you know my name? And who are you?'

'I'm sorry,' Mel said. 'I should have introduced you to one another.'

He knew that Cindy was wondering about his relationship with Tanya. She was looking at Tanya in a strange way. Had she already guessed that they planned to meet later that night? It didn't matter what she thought, though, now that they had decided to get divorced.

'How nice that attractive ladies come to ask you for your advice,' Cindy said sweetly. 'It must make your job so much more interesting.' She turned to Tanya. 'Now, what exactly was your problem?'

'I said that I wanted some advice.'

'Oh really? What kind of advice? Professional or personal?'

'Stop it, Cindy!' Mel said sharply. 'That's enough! You have no right to behave like this!'

Tanya looked at Cindy calmly. 'It's about Flight Two. That's a flight to Rome, Mrs Bakersfeld.'

'What's wrong?' Mel asked.

Tanya told him about the thin man with a small case, and her conversation with the Customs Officer, Standish.

'It sounds like a job for Italian Customs, not us,' he said.

They had both forgotten that Cindy was there.

'I'm not sure. I've checked on this man, and I've discovered something strange about him. He's flying to Rome without any luggage.'

'Flying to Rome without any luggage! That's mad! Why would he do that?'

'I don't know,' Tanya admitted, 'well – it may sound stupid, but . . .'

'Go on. What are you trying to suggest?'

'Perhaps he doesn't need any luggage because he knows that the flight will never arrive. If there's a bomb in the case–'

A bomb. Mel wondered what he should do. It could be all imagination and yet – what if it was true? He did not want to look a fool, but on the other hand . . . Then he thought of one thing that he could check.

He phoned the insurance desk, and asked the girl for the names of all the people who had bought flight insurance policies that evening.

While he was waiting for the girl to find the names, he asked Tanya: 'Did you get the name of the man with no luggage?'

'Yes, his name's Guerrero. D. O. Guerrero.'

The same name as that woman Ned Ordway had brought to his office! Could there be some connection?

'Tanya,' he said, 'there was a middle-aged woman waiting outside my office earlier this evening. I didn't have time to see her, and she left. Try and find her now. Her name is Inez Guerrero.'

Tanya went off to make the announcement that he hoped Inez Guerrero would hear. It would be heard all over the terminal.

The girl from the insurance desk came back to the telephone with the information that Mel needed. Now he knew exactly how important it was to find Inez.

They must find her. If only he had had time to talk to her earlier! But there had been the Meadowood meeting, and Keith to worry about – Mel remembered he had considered going back to the control tower. Then there had been Cindy. He looked around and realized that Cindy had gone. He had not even noticed her leaving.

He phoned Ordway. Now every policeman in the airport would be looking for Inez Guerrero.

Tanya came back. 'Have you discovered anything new about our man?' she asked.

Mel answered her slowly and quietly. 'Yes, I have. Guerrero, the man who is going to Rome without any luggage, insured his life this evening for three hundred thousand dollars. In the event of his death, the money would go to Inez Guerrero. He bought the policy with his last few coins.'

Tanya turned white. 'Oh no!' she whispered. 'Oh God, no!'

Chapter 29   The Plane on the Runway

Patroni was glad that he worked out on the airfield, and not in an office. He saw the office workers and managers as children who played games against one another. On the other hand, he saw the engineers and maintenance men as adults who shared their skills and worked together.

This was being proved to him tonight. He had begun the job of digging under the Aéreo-Mexican plane with a small group of Aéreo-Mexican and TWA workers. Now they were being helped by others from Braniff and Pan Am who had come without being asked. That made Patroni feel good.

In spite of the additional help, this job was taking longer than he had expected. The digging was progressing slowly, because the men had to stop very often to warm themselves. It was bitterly cold. When they had finished it would be the pilot's responsibility to drive the plane forwards, out of the wet ground.

Patroni had been digging too. He enjoyed sharing the work done by his team of men. Now he stopped and said: 'We'll be finished in five minutes. I'll go and talk to the pilot.'

The Mexican pilot was listening to music inside the plane. It was warm and comfortable in there. As Patroni came in, he turned the radio off.

'Don't worry,' Patroni said. 'Enjoy the music. We didn't really expect you to come and help us with our work.'

'I have my job to do. You have yours,' the captain said, in his correct but rather stiff English.

'Sure, but we all want to get this plane out of the mud. Would you like me to drive it out?'

'No thank you,' the captain said coldly.

'It will be very difficult, and I've done it before.'

'Mr Patroni, I know who you are. I am sure that you are very good at your job. But I am the captain of this plane, and I shall remain in control of it!'

'All right. But when I tell you to, make sure that you give the engines full power – and I mean full power!'

Patroni left the captain. Outside the digging had stopped. They were ready to move the plane.

'Ready to start!'

There was a sudden burst of noise as engine number three started.

'Clear to start four!'

The maintenance men were running out of the way of the plane.

'Clear to start two!'

'Clear to start one!'

Patroni was on the telephone to the captain. 'Let's get moving! More power!' he shouted, as the engines and the plane shook.

The engine noise grew, and then suddenly died.

'It cannot be done,' the captain said. 'If I give the engines more power, the plane will stand on its nose. Instead of a stuck plane we shall have a damaged one.'

'It can be done! It can, if you have the courage to try!'

'You may try now, if you like. Let us see what your courage can do. Will you accept full responsibility for this plane?'

'Yes!'

'Good night, then.'

As the pilot left, Patroni examined the ground beneath the plane. As he had feared, the plane was now deeper in the mud than before.

They would have to start the whole operation again a hard job to ask tired men to do. Patroni knew that he could move the plane. This time, he would take the controls.

Chapter 30   Inez Loses Hope

Inez Guerrero could no longer remember where she was or why she was there. Her troubles were too great for her to bear, and her tired brain refused to think any more.

The taxi-driver who had brought her to the airport had added to her pain. She had paid him with her last ten dollars, and expected him to give her some change. He said that he had none, but that he would go and get some. Inez wasted time by waiting for him. He never returned, and he had taken the last of her money.

If she had not waited for the change, she might have reached Gate 47 before Flight Two left. But she had been too late. She learned from the agent at the gate that D. O. Guerrero had left on Flight Two.

Now she was completely alone and without money. She began to cry. At first the tears came slowly. Then, as she thought of all her troubles, she began to cry noisily. She cried for the past and for the present, for what she had had and what she had lost. She cried for her home and children, and for her husband who had now left her. She cried because her shoes hurt her feet, because her clothes were wet, and because she felt old and tired and ill. She cried for herself and for everyone else who was poor and who lived without hope.

People began to give her strange looks, so she wandered away, without knowing where to go. Soon after, a policeman found her and took her to Mel's office. She did not understand where she was being taken, but she went quietly.

She sat there for a while, but then she wandered away again. Once, she thought she heard her name in an announcement, but she knew that she must be dreaming. Nobody at the airport could possibly know her name.

Chapter 31   Danger for the *Golden Argosy*

Several people were hurrying towards Mel's office as quickly as they could. Mel and Tanya had made some phone calls, and they had made it clear that speed was all important.

Bert Weatherby, the Transport Manager of TWA and Tanya's boss, arrived first, followed by Ned Ordway.

'What's this all about?' Weatherby asked.

'We're not sure, but we think there may be a bomb on board the Rome flight.'

Weatherby looked hard at Tanya, but he said nothing. Mel told the two men all that he and Tanya knew. While he was explaining the situation Harry Standish came in with Bunnie Vorobioff, the girl who had sold the insurance policy to Guerrero. As she listened to what Mel was saying, she began to look pale and frightened.

'What we have to decide,' Mel told them all, 'is whether we should warn the captain of Flight Two, and if so, what we should tell him.' The captain of Flight Two was Vernon Demerest, he remembered.

The telephone rang. There was more information for them about Flight Two, giving them the present position of the plane, and its height, speed and course. There was some news from Joe Patroni, too. Runway three zero would be out of use for at least one more hour.

Weatherby asked: 'That woman – the passenger's wife. What's her name?'

'Inez Guerrero,' Ordway told him.

'Where is she?'

'We don't know. My men are looking for her now.'

'She was here,' Mel said. 'We had no idea–'

'We were all slow,' Weatherby said.

Tanya knew that he was remembering that he had told her to 'forget it!' when she had tried to talk to him about Guerrero.

'Perhaps we should send a description of Guerrero to the captain,' she suggested.

'Yes,' Mel agreed. 'We have someone here who has seen him and can describe him.'

He turned to Bunnie. 'Are you Miss Vorobioff?'

All the men turned to look at her. Weatherby almost whistled, but he managed to stop himself just in time.

'Do you remember the man we are talking about?'

'I – I'm not sure,' she said nervously.

'A man called D. O. Guerrero. You sold him an insurance policy, didn't you?'

'Yes.'

'So you can tell us what he looks like.'

'No – I can't.'

Mel looked surprised. 'But I thought you said earlier that you could!'

'I'm sorry. I don't remember now.'

Ned Ordway stepped towards Bunnie. 'Listen,' he said. 'I know that you can describe this man. You're frightened, aren't you? You think that it will get you into trouble?'

Bunnie did not answer.

Ordway's voice was hard as he went on. 'You'll be in really big trouble if you refuse to tell us what you know. Now, I'll ask you once more. Do you remember Guerrero?'

'Yes,' she said quietly.

'Describe him.'

'A thin man with nervous hands. A pale yellowish face and thin lips. He had no Italian money, and had to search his pockets before he found enough coins to pay for his insurance policy.'

'And you sold him one!' Weatherby cried. 'You must be mad!'

'I thought—'

'You thought! But what did you do? Nothing! Oh, we're all mad to allow you to sell insurance at an airport.'

Mel turned to Standish. 'Would you like to say anything?'

'Just this. If this man has a bomb in his case, he must be able to reach it easily. If anyone is going to try to take the case from him, it will have to be done very carefully.'

'Of course,' Mel said, 'there may be no bomb. He may be just an ordinary passenger.'

'I don't think so. I wish I did, because my favourite little girl is on that flight.'

If only I had acted earlier! Standish was thinking. *How will I tell Judy's parents if anything happens to her?*

'As a Customs man, I'm used to watching people,' he went on. 'Let me say something about Guerrero. I'm sure that he's a dangerous man. Put that word in your message to the captain – *dangerous.*'

As the message was being prepared and sent, Ordway received some news from his men. They had found Inez Guerrero.

She had been sitting quietly in a corner when she heard someone ask: 'Inez Guerrero? Are you Mrs Inez Guerrero?'

She looked up and saw a policeman. A different policeman from last time.

'Are you Mrs Guerrero?'

'Yes,' she whispered.

'Come on. The whole airport's looking for you.'

Ten minutes later she was sitting in Mel's office, surrounded by people.

'Mrs Guerrero,' Ordway asked, 'why is your husband going to Rome?'

She did not answer.

'Please listen to me carefully. We need your help. I have to ask you some questions about your husband. Will you answer them?'

'Come on!' Weatherby said impatiently. 'This is wasting time. Get rough with her if you have to!'

'Leave it to me, Mr Weatherby,' Ordway said calmly, 'Shouting won't make this any quicker.'

'Inez,' he continued. 'May I call you Inez?'

'Yes,' she whispered.

'Inez, will you answer my questions?'

'Yes – if I can.'

'Why is your husband going to Rome?'

He could hardly hear her answer. 'I don't know.'

'Have you got any friends there?'

'No.'

'What is your husband's job?'

'He was a builder.'

'Was? Isn't he now?'

'Things went – wrong.'

'Is he in trouble?'

'Yes.'

'In debt?'

'Yes.'

'Then how did he pay for his ticket?'

She told Ordway about the ring that D. O. had sold.

'Did you agree to this?'

'No! I didn't know what he was doing.'

'I believe you, Inez. Did your husband often do strange things without telling you?'

'Yes.'

'Was he ever violent?'

'Yes,' she whispered. 'Please, why do you want to know all this?'

'Did he ever use explosives?'

'Yes – he liked using them.'

Everyone in the room was suddenly silent.

'Where do you live?'

She gave them her address.

'And where did he keep the explosives?'

'In a drawer in the bedroom.' A sudden look of shock crossed her face.

Ordway saw it. 'You thought of something then! What was it?'

'Nothing.'

'That's not true! Tell me, Inez, what was it?' Ordway had stopped being gentle and polite. Now he was shouting 'Tell me! Tell me!' at her.

'Tonight – the explosives – I didn't think of it before.'

'Yes! Go on!'

'They had gone.'

Nobody spoke.

'Did you know that your husband was going to insure his life heavily?'

'No – no–'

'I believe you. Now listen to me carefully. We think that your husband intends to use those explosives to blow up the plane he is on. He is heavily insured, and the money would come to you. The explosion would kill everyone on the plane – including children. Inez, you know your husband. Could he do a thing like that?'

Tears poured down her face. She could hardly speak. 'Yes,' she cried. 'Yes, I think he could.'

Chapter 32   Vernon's Plan

On board the *Golden Argosy* Captains Harris and Demerest were enjoying a good meal. They had exactly the same to eat as the first-class passengers, but without the wine, of course.

Suddenly, their meal was interrupted as a radio message came through. While Vernon wrote it down, his face changed. He passed it to Harris and Jordan.

There was only one sensible thing to do – turn in a wide circle that the passengers would not notice, and return to Lincoln International. Harris began to do this immediately. Vernon sent for Gwen.

'What do you want?' she asked as she came in. 'If it's more to eat, I'll have to say no!'

'We want you to look for a passenger,' Vernon told her. 'Look, you'd better read this message.'

As she stood by him reading, he watched her face. She looked serious, but not frightened. He remembered that she had told him that she loved him. He wondered whether he himself had ever really loved anybody. Perhaps what he felt for Gwen was the nearest that he would ever come to love.

For a moment he felt angry about the change in plans. They would not get to Naples now as quickly as he would have liked to. A second later he was the complete professional pilot once again, with thoughts only for his plane and his passengers.

'Find this man, Gwen,' he told her. 'See how easy it would be to get the case from him.'

'I've already noticed him,' she said quietly. 'I don't need to look again. He wouldn't let me touch his case when I took him his dinner. Another reason I remember him is that he's sitting next to our old lady stowaway. He's between her and the window.'

'That will make it difficult for us to get the case away from him.'

For the first time Vernon began to feel that they were in danger.

'If only we could think of some trick,' he said slowly. 'Did you say that he's next to our little old stowaway?'

'Yes.'

'And she doesn't yet know that we know who she is?'

'That's right.'

'Listen. I have an idea. It may work.'

◆

Mrs Quonsett was just finishing her meal. 'That was very nice, my dear,' she said to the girl who had come to clear the empty meal containers.

Then she noticed another girl standing by her. She had black hair, an intelligent face, and strong, dark eyes. Mrs Quonsett had noticed her earlier.

'Excuse me. May I see your ticket?'

'Why, of course,' Mrs Quonsett said. She knew what was happening, but she never gave up without a fight.

She pretended to search her handbag. 'How strange! I simply can't seem to find my ticket!'

'Shall I look?' Gwen said coldly. 'If you have a ticket, I'm sure I'll find it.'

'Certainly not! My handbag is private. I shall find the ticket myself. You're English, aren't you?' she went on. 'How beautiful you make our language sound. My husband always used to say–'

'Never mind about him. I want your ticket.' It was hard for Gwen to be so rude and unpleasant to an old woman, but Vernon had told her exactly what she had to do.

'I'm trying to be patient with you, my dear, but I really shall have to complain.'

'Will you, Mrs Quonsett? You see, I know all about you. This isn't the first plane you've got on without a ticket, is it?'

'If you know all about me already, there's nothing more I can say.'

'What's wrong?' Mrs Quonsett's musician friend asked. 'Perhaps I can help.'

'Are you travelling with this lady?'

'No.'

'Then this does not concern you.'

'Are we going back to the airport?' Mrs Quonsett asked.

'You're not important enough for that. We'll deal with you in Rome.'

Gwen hoped that Guerrero was listening. She looked at him quickly, and felt a sudden icy fear.

'Come with me,' she said to the old lady. 'The captain wants to speak to you, and he doesn't like to be kept waiting.'

Mrs Quonsett was feeling rather frightened of the captain, so she was very surprised when he said 'Hello!' to her in a friendly voice.

'Forget what happened just then,' he told her. 'I ordered Miss Meighen to be rude to you. That isn't the reason I want to speak to you.'

Mrs Quonsett looked around. How exciting to see how a plane was flown! It would be another adventure to tell her daughter about.

'Do you get frightened easily?' the captain asked her.

What a strange question! 'No,' she said. 'When you are as old as I am, there isn't much left to be frightened of.'

'We need your help, Mrs Quonsett,' he told her. 'I suppose you've noticed the man sitting between you and the window?'

'Yes. He won't talk to anyone. I think he's worried about something.'

'We're worried, too. We think that he has a bomb in his case.'

This was exciting, but a bit frightening, too.

'I suppose you want me to try and take the case away from him,' she said.

'No! Don't touch the case. That would be very dangerous for us all. Now listen . . .'

When he had finished telling her his plan, she smiled. 'Oh yes, I think I can do that,' she said.

'Why do you keep flying to New York as a stowaway?' Vernon asked her. She told him all about her daughter in New York, and how lonely she sometimes felt in San Diego.

'If you can help us now,' he said, 'I promise we'll give you a free ticket to New York and back, first class.'

Mrs Quonsett's eyes filled with tears. How kind! What a dear, wonderful man!

◆

Mrs Quonsett really was crying as Gwen pushed her roughly back towards her seat. 'What a good actress I'm becoming!' she thought happily.

'Couldn't you be less rough?' one passenger asked Gwen.

'Keep out of this, sir,' she replied, knowing that Guerrero could hear her. Again, she felt a wave of fear at the thought of him.

As Mrs Quonsett's friendly neighbour stood up to let her sit down, Gwen stood between him and his seat. Vernon was waiting behind the curtain between the first-class and tourist areas, ready to come in when his help was needed.

Still standing, Mrs Quonsett began to beg Gwen: 'Please, ask the captain to change his mind! I don't want to go to prison!'

'I don't give orders to the captain!' Gwen shouted. 'Now sit down!'

Ada Quonsett began to cry noisily. 'Please take me home! Don't leave me in a strange country!'

'How can you be so cruel to this old lady?' the musician complained to Gwen.

Gwen took no notice of him, but gave the old woman a hard push, so that she fell into her seat. 'You hurt me!' she cried. She turned to D. O. Guerrero. 'Help me! Help me!' He took no notice of her.

Crying and shouting, she threw her arms around his neck. He struggled with her, fighting to free himself, but she wound her arms around his neck more tightly. 'Oh, help me!'

Red-faced and breathless, D. O. Guerrero put up both hands to push her away. As if to beg him for help, she seized them. In a second Gwen had reached over and taken the case from him. It had all been surprisingly easy.

Vernon hurried in. 'Well done, Gwen. Let me take the case.'

That should have been the end of the whole affair. But it was not – and all because of a man called Marcus Rathbone.

He was an unpleasant man who always liked to criticize other people's ideas, although he had never had a good idea of his own in his life. He was especially critical of women. When he saw a woman in uniform take a man's case from him, he knew that he had to help that man. He seized the case from Gwen, and handed it politely back to Guerrero.

Like a wild animal, with madness in his eyes, Guerrero took it and held it tightly to him.

Vernon ran forwards, but he was too late. Gwen, Rathbone and the musician were in his way, and he could not reach Guerrero before he had pushed past them and was rushing down the plane.

'Stop that man!' Vernon shouted. 'He has a bomb!'

Everywhere, passengers were jumping to their feet, shouting.

Guerrero stopped with his back to the toilets. 'Stay away from me!' he shouted.

'Guerrero, listen to me!' Vernon called to him over the heads of the others. 'Do you hear me? Listen!'

There was silence as Guerrero looked back at him, his eyes wild.

'We know who you are,' Vernon went on, 'and we know what you're trying to do. We know all about the insurance and the bomb, and they know about it back at the airport, too. That means that the insurance is no good. Do you understand? It's worth nothing. If you die, you'll die for nothing and your family will get nothing. Worse than that, they'll be blamed and made to suffer. Think of that, Guerrero.'

A woman cried out. Guerrero paused.

Vernon knew that he had to keep talking, and hope that Guerrero would listen to what he had to say.

'Guerrero, let's all sit down. I'd like to talk to you. Nobody on this plane's going to hurt you, I promise.'

Gwen was closest to Guerrero.

'Try to get into a seat,' Vernon whispered to Gwen. 'I may have to move quickly.'

A man came out of one of the toilets behind Guerrero. At the sound of the door opening, Guerrero turned.

'Get the man with the case! He's got a bomb!' somebody shouted.

Guerrero pushed past the man and ran into the toilet. Gwen had run after him, and she stuck her foot in the door as he tried to close it.

Guerrero had not really understood everything that had happened in the last few minutes, but he understood that, like so many other things in his life, his great plan had failed. His life had

101

been a failure, and now his death would be a failure too.

As he pulled the string, he wondered bitterly whether the bomb would be another failure. In the last second of his life he learned that it was not.

Chapter 33   Emergency in the Air

The explosion on board Flight Two was immediate. Inside the plane there was a sudden noise like thunder, or a blow from a great hammer. A sheet of flame shot along the length of the plane.

D. O. Guerrero died at once. His body was near the centre of the explosion, and was completely destroyed. One moment he existed; the next moment only a few small bloody pieces of flesh remained.

A large hole appeared in the side of the plane.

Gwen Meighen was nearest to Guerrero, and received the force of the explosion in her face and chest.

The hole in the side of the plane caused an immediate change in the air pressure. A dark, terrible cloud of dust rolled through the plane, carrying newspapers, bottles and bags towards the hole. Curtains and doors were torn off and thrown about the plane, hitting several people and adding to the confusion. Passengers held onto their seats to avoid being sucked out of the plane. Oxygen lines fell down on them from the emergency containers above their heads.

Suddenly the sucking stopped. The plane filled with mist, and a freezing, deadly cold. The noise from the engines and the wind was unbelievably loud.

Vernon Demerest had held onto a seat, seized an oxygen line and shouted: 'Get on oxygen!' to the passengers. He knew that after only ten seconds without enough oxygen, their lives would be in danger.

He had to get back to Harris and Jordan to tell them what had happened. Breathing deeply, he moved from one oxygen line to the next. As he went, he noticed a young girl helping the people next to her connect an oxygen line to their baby. He found out later that this was Judy, and Standish was her uncle.

Vernon had no time to think of Gwen. He did not even know whether she was alive or dead. Before he could reach Harris, the plane suddenly began dropping fast.

◆

Harris and Jordan did not know exactly what had happened, but they had felt the shock of the explosion, and the pressure change which followed it. The door to the pilots' area was torn off and a thick cloud of dust rushed in. As in the passenger part of the plane, this had been replaced by a fine mist and a terrible cold.

Harris acted quickly, using all his skill and experience in his fight to save the plane. Fortunately, like all pilots, he had practised dealing with emergencies so often that when a real emergency came, he acted with the greatest speed.

It was a rule of aviation that, in an emergency, airline employees must take care of themselves before they began to think about the passengers. Harris reached for an oxygen line immediately, and a moment later Cy Jordan pressed the button that gave the passengers the oxygen they needed.

Harris reduced the speed of the plane. Now he had a decision to make. It was necessary to take the plane down to a safer height where they could breathe without the help of oxygen. The question was, should he bring the plane down slowly, or in a rapid fall?

If the plane was badly damaged, a sudden fall could break it in two. But if they went down slowly, there was a chance that the passengers would die of the cold. What could they do? Freeze for certain, or take a risk and go down fast?

'Warn Air Traffic Control,' Harris told Jordan. 'We're coming down fast.'

He pushed the controls forward. 'We are coming down fast,' he heard Jordan say. 'Request 10,000 feet.'

They were falling rapidly. Passing through 26,000 feet – 24 – 23. There was no other traffic near them. No time to think about the cold. They would live – if they could get low enough fast enough – if the plane did not break up. At fourteen thousand feet, Harris decided, he would pull out of the fall, and level at ten.

The controls were stiff and heavy, but everything seemed to be working. They were coming out of the fall. Eleven thousand feet – ten five – ten. They were level. The plane had not broken up. He had made the right decision.

Now they needed information from Toronto. Where could they land – at Detroit, Toronto or Lincoln International?

Vernon Demerest came in.

'We missed you,' Harris said.

'How're we doing?'

'If the tail doesn't fall off, we may be all right. What happened?'

'Oh, just a little bomb that made a big hole in our nice plane.'

They did not want to talk about the real dangers of the situation.

'It was a good idea, Vernon,' Harris said kindly. 'It could have worked.'

'Yes, but it didn't.'

Vernon told Jordan to go and see how bad the damage was.

'Count the people who are hurt and do what you can to help them,' he said. 'And find out how badly hurt Gwen is.' It was the first time that he had allowed himself to think about her.

Toronto Air Traffic Control Centre reported that Detroit and Toronto airports were closed, but Lincoln was still open. Carrying the large amount of fuel that they were, landing anywhere would be difficult. They needed the longest runway that they could get. That was at Lincoln – an hour's flying time away. The question was, could the plane stay in the air for another hour?

Jordan reported on the damage. He thought that the plane would be able to reach Lincoln, but he was not so sure about the passengers. There were several doctors working among them.

'What about Gwen?' Vernon asked, afraid as he spoke of what the answer might be. The news was not encouraging. She was more badly hurt than anyone else.

'We'll land at Lincoln,' Captain Harris decided.

Runway three zero was the one that they wanted. It was still blocked by the Aéreo-Mexican plane.

'They have 50 minutes to clear it for us,' Vernon said roughly. 'They'll have to clear it. It's our only chance.'

Chapter 34   The People from Meadowood

Elliott Freemantle could not understand it. A large number of people from the Meadowood meeting had followed him to the airport, and were at the moment making a great deal of noise in the main hall of the terminal. Television cameras had arrived, but there were no policemen! Elliott wanted the police to arrive. Then there would be trouble – and a big story for the press.

All the time he was talking to the television reporters, he was waiting for the police to arrive.

'Why are you here?' a reporter asked him.

'Because this airport is full of thieves and liars.'

'That's strong talk. Will you explain exactly what you mean by it?'

'Certainly. The peace, the rest and the good health of these people are being stolen from them by this airport. Nobody cares how much they suffer. Only this evening the airport manager told them that the noise will get worse, not better! He didn't care.'

'What are you going to do about this?'

'We're going to take the airport to court – to the highest court in the land, if necessary. We shall begin by asking for some runways – if not the whole airport – to be closed at night. I care about these people! I shall fight for them, and I shall win!'

The crowd was growing bigger all the time, Elliott noticed, and people were growing angrier too. When he had finished speaking, a man shouted: 'Let's show the airport how loud a noise can be!' and a great shout rose from the throats of the crowd. If the police came now, the press would certainly write about the meeting.

What Elliott Freemantle did not know was that every policeman in the airport was looking for Inez Guerrero. Even after she had been found, Ordway, the police chief, was busy talking to her in Mel's office. When he had finished, he and Mel left the office together.

Immediately they saw Elliott Freemantle surrounded by a crowd of people and cameras.

'That lawyer again!' Ordway said. 'I'll soon get rid of him!'

'Be careful,' Mel said. 'He wants attention from the press. We don't want to help him.'

As Ordway went to speak to the lawyer, Mel saw Tomlinson, the young reporter he had met earlier that evening. He asked him what Elliott had been saying, and when he found out his face darkened with anger.

'Freemantle!' he shouted, 'I'm interested in what you've been saying this evening. Do these people know that it's all lies?'

Everyone was silent. They turned to look at Mel.

'Don't listen to him!' Elliott shouted.

'I think that the press should hear what I have to say,' Mel said. 'I'm the airport manager. Mr Freemantle has told you that I don't care how much these people are suffering. Now I'd like to answer that criticism.'

'He'll tell you more lies!'

'You be quiet!' Ned Ordway told Elliott. 'You've spoken already. Now listen!'

Mel spoke for the second time that evening about how they tried to reduce noise at the airport, and how the storm had made it necessary to use the runway nearest to Meadowood. Again he said that planes were becoming bigger and noisier all the time.

'I do care about your problem,' he went on, 'but I must remind you of something. You won't like listening to this, but it's true.'

Twelve years ago, the land where their houses now stood had been empty. Building companies had been told not to use it for houses, but some of them had been too interested in money to take any notice of the warnings. They had built houses and sold them to people without telling them that the noise from planes would be getting worse and worse. These builders, and not the airport, were to blame for the present problem.

Nobody spoke. Mel felt very sorry for the people who had bought houses in Meadowood. They were just ordinary people, and he wished that he could help them.

'Now,' he said, 'there are some lawyers who are making a lot of money for themselves out of people with the same problem as you have. They're cheating you.'

'That isn't true! He's lying!' Elliott shouted, but the crowd seemed to want to listen to Mel.

He told them that they had very little chance of winning their case against the airport. People had won, it was true, but those cases had been very different. He told them about some other cases which had failed.

Now the anger of the crowd turned against Elliott Freemantle.

'How can we get our money back?' they began to ask. 'We were fools to sign anything too quickly.'

'Write to Mr Freemantle immediately,' Mel told them. 'Tell him that you've changed your mind. I don't think that you'll hear from him again.'

Elliott knew it was the end. He never went on fighting when he knew that he had no chance of winning. Ah well, he would soon find some more fools in another town, he was sure.

As the Meadowood people went sadly and quietly home, a woman came up to Mel.

'Thank you for talking to us and for telling us the truth,' she said, 'but I still don't know what I can tell my children when they can't sleep because of the noise.'

Mel knew that there was nothing he could say to her. That was the saddest thing about the whole affair.

As he was wondering what to say, Tanya handed him a piece of paper. From it he learned of the explosion on board the *Golden Argosy*. The plane would have to land at Lincoln International on runway three zero. And runway three zero was still blocked.

Chapter 35   Return to Lincoln Airport

Doctor Milton Compagno was doing his best to save Gwen Meighen's life.

She had been near to the centre of the explosion. Two things –

108

the toilet door and Guerrero's body – had been between her and the full force of the explosion, and they had saved her life.

Now she lay on the floor, unconscious and bleeding. Some of the passengers were also bleeding from cuts, but they were not seriously hurt in comparison with Gwen.

It was fortunate that as she fell her arm had fallen around the base of a seat. If this had not happened, she might have been sucked out of the hole in the side of the plane.

The next great danger was from lack of oxygen. Some people managed to get to the oxygen quickly and then help others, as Vernon had seen Judy do. Mrs Quonsett, too, had helped her musician friend to get oxygen. She did not really care whether she lived or died – as long as she knew what was happening until the last moment!

Gwen received no oxygen. When Anson Harris put the plane into a fall, he saved her from certain death from lack of oxygen.

After the plane levelled out again, everyone began to think they might be over the worst. The three doctors who were travelling on the flight started to do what they could to help those who had been hurt.

It was lucky for Gwen that there was a man like Compagno on board. He seemed to enjoy helping people, and since he had become a doctor he had never stopped working. Of the three doctors on the plane he was the only one who had a medical bag with him.

He directed the other doctors to look after the passengers, and to move those who had been hurt to the front of the plane, where it was warmer. Then he asked one of the air hostesses to help him, and gave Gwen some oxygen. He cleared blood and broken teeth from her mouth, and began to control the bleeding from her face and chest. One arm was broken, but what worried him most was the damage to her left eye.

When Cy Jordan came to see how Gwen was, Compagno

asked him to help for a few minutes before he told him: 'She has a good chance, if she's a strong girl.'

'I think she's strong,' Jordan said.

'She was a pretty girl, wasn't she?'

'Very.'

Compagno was silent. She would not be pretty any more.

Looking a little sicker than before, Jordan went forward to the pilots' area.

Vernon Demerest made an announcement to the passengers. 'As you know,' he said, 'we're in trouble – bad trouble. But we're still alive, and we hope to make a safe landing at Lincoln International in about 45 minutes. It will be a difficult landing, so you must all help us by doing exactly what we tell you to do. Let's try and come through this together – safely.'

'That was good,' Harris said. 'You ought to be in politics!'

'Nobody would vote for me. They don't like to hear the truth. It hurts them too much.' He was thinking about the matter of the sale of flight insurance at the airport, and wondering how Mel Bakersfeld would feel about it after what had happened tonight. He didn't suppose that Mel would ever change his closed little mind. Well, if he lived through this, Vernon would continue to fight him with all his strength!

A radio message came through. Lincoln's runway three zero was still out of use, but they were trying to clear it. Vernon's face showed clearly what he thought of that!

He sent Jordan back to talk to the passengers and make sure that they knew what to do before the landing. As Jordan left, Doctor Compagno came in.

'Your Miss Meighen is the most badly hurt,' he told Vernon. 'Can you radio for a doctor to be waiting for her at the airport? Her left eye will need immediate treatment.'

Vernon went pale with shock as the doctor described her wounds. He felt sick.

'I'd better go back to her now,' Compagno said.

'Don't go!'

Compagno looked surprised.

'Gwen – Miss Meighen – she was – is – going to have a baby. Does it make any difference?'

'I didn't know that, but, no, it won't make any difference. If she lives, the baby should be all right.'

There was a silence until Harris said: 'Vernon, could you fly for a bit? I'd like to rest before I make the landing.'

Vernon was glad to have something to do. He was also glad that Harris had not asked any questions about Gwen.

He could not stop thinking about her. She had been so beautiful, and she had told him that she loved him. Now she had only 'a good chance' of living. She might never see Naples.

Suddenly he knew that he loved her. There could be no question of giving the baby away or of her having an abortion now. She would have the baby, and he would take full responsibility for it.

He remembered his daughter, the child he had never seen. Before her birth he had wanted to tell Sarah about her, and suggest that they should have her as part of their family, but he had not had the courage. Now he often wondered where she was and whether she was happy. He had even tried to find her, but it had not been possible.

He would not suffer the same uncertainty again over this child. This time it would all be different. He would not lie to Sarah. Oh, there would be the most terrible trouble at home! There would be crying and shouting. But Sarah was a sensible woman, and he knew that she would not leave him. He would have two women and a baby to look after. What a terrible situation! But he was glad that he had made a decision.

He began to think about the baby. Perhaps it would be rather nice to be a father! Not that he would want to have seven children like that old fool Harris! He laughed.

'What are you laughing at?' Harris asked.

'Laughing? Why should I be laughing? There must be something wrong with your ears, Anson. You should see a doctor about it.'

'There's no need to be unpleasant,' Harris said.

'Isn't there? I think that's exactly what we need in this situation – someone to be unpleasant!'

'Well, if that's what we need, I'm sure you're the best man for the job.'

Harris took control of the plane again. As he did so, Vernon sent a radio message to Toronto. Anson Harris was right – he was good at being unpleasant.

'Are you listening there, or are you all asleep? Tell Lincoln we need runway three zero. Don't tell me it's still blocked; I've heard that before. If we land anywhere else, we'll have a broken plane full of dead people. So get me three zero, do you understand?'

Then he added a special message for Mel Bakersfeld: 'You helped to get us into this situation, you stupid fool, by not listening to me about selling flight insurance at the airport. Now help us to get out of it. Wake up for once in your useless life, and get that runway clear!'

Chapter 36   The Runway Stays Blocked

Through the radio in his fast-moving car, Mel could hear emergency vehicles being called out onto the airfield. They had to be there to deal with the possibility of fire, and to take the people who had been hurt off the plane.

He received some information about Patroni. He hoped to be able to move the Aéreo-Mexican plane in 20 minutes.

Tanya and Tomlinson were with Mel in the car. The reporter

had helped Mel earlier, by telling him what Elliott Freemantle was doing, and now Mel wanted to help him to get a good story.

'Let me check something,' Tomlinson said. 'There's only one runway long enough for this plane to land safely on. Is that right?'

'Yes,' Mel said. 'There should be two.' He had been trying for years to persuade the Airport Committee that another runway of that length was needed. They would not take any notice of him – for political reasons, as he well knew.

'May I put all this in my story?' the reporter asked.

Mel paused for a moment. 'Why not?' he said.

'You've been speaking well tonight, if I may say so,' Tomlinson went on. 'Just like you used to a few years ago.'

Just like I used to, Mel thought. Not like I do now. People know that I've changed, that I've lost something.

'You're talking about how you need more runways,' Tanya said, 'but I keep thinking about the people on that plane. I can't help wondering how they feel, and if they're frightened.'

'They're frightened,' Mel said. 'If they understand what's happening, they must be frightened.' He remembered his own crash, long ago. As he thought of it, the pain in his foot returned.

It was then that the first radio message from Vernon Demerest came through.

'There's another message, Mr Bakersfeld, for you alone. It's rather personal. Do you want to hear it?'

'Does it concern the present situation?'

'Yes.'

'Then read it.'

They listened in silence. Vernon must have enjoyed sending that, Mel thought. He knew that people all over the airport would be able to hear it. In any case, the message was unnecessary. Mel had already decided what he had to do.

He spoke to Danny Farrow. 'Send the snowploughs and heavy

vehicles to the stuck plane. If Patroni can't drive the plane out very soon, we'll push it out. I'll give the order myself.'

'All right,' Danny said, his voice tired. 'Mel, I suppose you know what those vehicles will do to a plane?'

'They'll move it,' Mel replied sharply, 'and that's the most important thing.'

'Move it!' Tomlinson exclaimed. 'They'll break it into little pieces! You'll break up a six million dollar plane!'

'I know, but we may have to do it to save lives. I hope not.'

Tanya reached for Mel's hand. 'You're doing the right thing,' she said. 'Remember that.'

Mel got out of his car near the stuck plane, and spoke to a very cold and tired Joe Patroni. He told him what he planned to do.

'Push an undamaged plane with snowploughs!' Patroni exploded. 'You're mad!'

'We may have to do it, Joe.'

'Listen, I'll drive it out in 15 minutes! Just give me a little more time.'

'I will,' Mel said, 'but when Ground Control gives you the order to stop, you must stop.'

The three of them sat in the car, waiting. Tomlinson was thinking about his story. 'Has what is happening made you change your ideas about flight insurance?' he asked Mel.

'Couldn't you ask that question some other time?' Tanya said angrily, but Mel said: 'I'll answer it now. I may have to change my mind, but I don't know yet. I'm still thinking about it.'

The minutes passed slowly. Now there was time for Tomlinson to ask all the questions about aviation that he had wanted to ask earlier. It helped to pass the time for Mel.

Suddenly Tanya cried: 'Look! He's starting the engines!' The three of them fixed their eyes on the plane. It was not moving yet. There were six minutes left.

The noise of the engines grew. 'He's using all the engines now,'

114

Tanya said, 'but it isn't moving. Oh, I can't bear it!'

No, Patroni could not move it. Mel was ready to give the order to bring in the snowploughs. They would have to push the plane off the runway.

Chapter 37   Bringing Down Flight Two

Usually Air Traffic Control was quiet after midnight, but tonight was different. Because of the storm, flights were arriving very late, and Wayne Tevis and Keith were still on duty.

Keith was trying to think of his work and nothing but his work. In some strange way, his mind seemed to be working on two levels. On one level he directed the air traffic with something of his old skill; on the other level his thoughts were all about his personal problems. He felt that he had already left his family and friends for ever. He belonged now to the dead – to the Redfern family whose deaths he had caused. Soon he would be joining them . . .

Realization of what was happening on board Trans America Flight Two came to Keith gradually.

Wayne Tevis had been told all about the emergency. He knew that Vernon Demerest had asked for runway three zero to be cleared, but there was a possibility that it would not be clear in time. If that happened, the plane would have to land on two five. Radio communication had been set up between the control tower and Joe Patroni on board the Aéreo-Mexican plane.

Tevis wondered if he should send Keith off duty, or at least ask him to move. Where he was working now, he would be the one to control the landing of Flight Two. He decided to leave Keith where he was, but to stay close to him in case he needed help.

A number of radio messages made the situation clear to Keith. He heard Captain Demerest emphazise the importance of clearing three zero — or there would be 'a broken plane full of dead people'. He heard Vernon's message to Mel, too. He knew that Patroni was trying to move the plane, and that time was running out.

As the time when Flight Two was to land came nearer, Keith began to feel frightened. He did not want to do this! He couldn't do it! If he made a mistake, he would have a plane 'full of dead people' on his conscience. It had happened to him before.

Mel Bakersfeld, someone said, was ready to break up the Aéreo-Mexican plane in order to clear runway three zero.

The flower-like double signal of a plane in trouble appeared on the edge of the radar screen — unmistakably Trans America Flight Two. Keith looked around for Tevis. *He couldn't do it!*

He opened his mouth to call Tevis, but no words would come. It was like all the bad dreams that he had suffered from since the day when the Redferns had died.

He heard voices. They were waiting for him to reply, but he could say nothing. Where was Tevis? Suddenly, Keith felt a terrible anger — against his father, who had pushed him into this job; against Mel, who always seemed to be so successful; against Tevis; against everyone in this airport that he hated.

Somehow, the anger seemed to free his voice. 'Trans America Two,' he said, 'this is Lincoln. Sorry we kept you waiting. We're hoping to give you runway three zero. We'll know in three to five minutes if it's clear.'

Keith had no thought for anything but his work now. He would bring Flight Two down safely.

Mel had given the order for the vehicles to move in. Patroni had been told to get out of their way.

Chapter 38   Joe Patroni Tries Again

Joe Patroni knew that time was running out. He had not started the engines of the Aéreo-Mexican 707 until the last possible moment, so that his men could continue the work of clearing the snow around the plane.

When he realized that he could not wait any longer, he had a final look at the ground around the plane. He did not like what he saw. They needed to work for another 15 minutes, but they simply did not have that time.

He climbed into the plane, and shouted to Ingram: 'Get everybody out of the way! I'm starting the engines.' Men ran out from under the plane.

Snow was still falling, but it was lighter now.

Patroni called again: 'Send someone to help me up here – someone thin! I don't want to make this plane any heavier.'

Through the window he could see Mel's car, and behind it a line of snowploughs and heavy vehicles. When Mel had told him that he might have to push the plane off the runway with these vehicles, Patroni had been shocked. He found it hard to believe that anyone could destroy a fine machine on purpose. It was not that he did not care about the people on board the *Golden Argosy*; it was just that he loved planes, and could not bear to think that this one would be destroyed.

A young mechanic ran over to the plane. 'What's your name, son?' Patroni asked.

'Rolling, sir.'

Patroni laughed. 'We're trying to get this plane rolling! Perhaps you'll bring us luck!'

'Ready to start,' Ingram called.

Patroni started the engines, number three first, and then four, two and one. The noise grew louder and louder.

'Hold on, son!' Patroni told Rolling.

117

He increased the power. To their left he could see Mel Bakersfeld's car, and he knew that they had only a few minutes left.

The plane shook, but it did not move. The young mechanic looked worried.

'Come on!' Patroni exclaimed. 'Let's go!'

'Mr Patroni!' Rolling warned, 'we can't do it!'

Then the radio message came: 'Joe Patroni on board Aéreo-Mexican. This is Ground Control. We have a message from Mr Bakersfeld: There is no more time. Stop all engines. Repeat – stop all engines.'

Patroni said nothing.

'Mr Patroni!' Rolling shouted. 'Do you hear? We have to stop!'

'Can't hear you,' Patroni shouted. 'Too noisy in here.' There's always more time left than those people in Ground Control will admit, he thought. If only he had a cigar! He needed one badly, but his pocket was empty. Mel Bakersfeld had promised him a box if he could move this plane, he remembered.

He pushed the controls to their limit. The radio seemed to be going mad. All around them lights were flashing.

Suddenly the plane moved forwards. At first it moved slowly. Then it gained speed, and shot down the runway. Patroni brought it neatly to rest 200 feet from the runway. Three zero was clear and open – and there would be another story to tell about Joe Patroni.

Chapter 39 Landing

Trans America Flight Two, the *Golden Argosy*, was 10 miles from Lincoln, in cloud, at 1,500 feet.

Anson Harris was back at the controls as they were guided in by Lincoln Air Traffic Control. Vernon thought that he knew the controller's voice, but he could not think who it was.

Just before they landed, Doctor Compagno came to tell them: 'I thought you would like to know, Miss Meighen is doing quite well. If we can get her to hospital quickly, I think she'll live.'

Vernon found it impossible to speak, and it was Anson Harris who said: 'Thank you, doctor. We'll be landing in a few minutes.'

The passengers had been prepared for the landing. Two of the doctors were on either side of Gwen, ready to support her as they landed.

Mrs Quonsett was feeling rather frightened at last, and was holding her neighbour's hand tightly. She was tired. So much had happened to her in the last 24 hours. The captain had thanked her for her help, and had promised her a free first-class trip to New York and back. What a kind and wonderful man he was, she thought. The only thing was – would she be alive to take the free trip?

Judy was still helping her neighbours with their baby. The child was sleeping peacefully, with no idea of the danger it was in.

They were flying at 170 miles an hour. The weight of the plane meant that they would lose speed slowly after touching down on the runway, so that an extremely long runway was necessary for their safety.

Keith Bakersfeld's voice announced: 'Runway three zero is open.'

'Thank heavens!' Vernon said. 'At the very last moment!'

'We're going in low,' Harris said.

Vernon was looking out into the clouds and darkness, trying to see the airport lights. He was thinking of the great danger that they were all in. The landing would be heavy and fast, and there was a chance that the tail of the plane might break off. If it does, he thought, we're all dead. That man who made the bomb – what a pity he died! I'd like to tear him to pieces with my own hands!

They were coming down at 90 feet a minute. Harris was doing everything perfectly, but Vernon still wished that he could be at the controls. 'You must live, Gwen!' he said softly to himself. He knew that somehow they would find a way through their difficulties.

The plane came out of the clouds, and they could see the runway lights ahead of them.

'Clear to land,' Keith's voice said. 'Good luck, and out.'

They sped over the edge of the airfield. To the two pilots, the runway had never looked shorter.

They were above the runway now, and still moving at great speed. They were down, heavily. The end of the runway seemed to be rushing towards them. Beyond it lay snow and darkness.

Then they were slowing down. The darkness came nearer and nearer. The plane stopped, just 3 feet from the end of the runway.

Chapter 40   Keith Says Goodbye

In the radar room, Keith Bakersfeld looked at the clock and knew that he should remain on duty for another half-hour. He did not care.

He stood up and looked around. 'Tevis,' he said, 'I'm going. Thank you for trying to help me. Goodbye.'

He walked out of the room for ever, knowing that he should have done this years ago. He felt extremely happy. He had brought Flight Two down safely, and that would be his last job in Air Traffic Control.

He went to the small rest room where he kept his food and his coat. He took the photograph of Natalie out of his pocket, as he had done earlier that night. When he looked at her smiling face, he wanted to cry. He put the photograph back in his pocket. He would never come back to this room again.

It was at that moment he came to a new decision. He was not going back to the hotel, but home to Natalie. He knew that he would never work again in aviation, and that he would have to live with his memories. He would never be able to forget little Valerie and her death – but he would live. The Redferns were dead. Nothing could change that. But his own family was alive, and he was going to them now.

As he walked to his car, he threw the Nembutal into the snow.

Chapter 41   The End of the Storm

Mel Bakersfeld watched from his car as Flight Two landed and stopped safely at the end of the runway. The airport's emergency vehicles raced towards it.

Tanya and Tomlinson were going back to the terminal with Joe Patroni. Tanya would be needed at Gate 47 when the passengers were brought off the plane. Before she left, she asked Mel: 'Are you still coming to my apartment?'

'If it isn't too late,' he said, 'I'd like to.'

She pushed her red hair off her face with one hand and smiled at him. 'It isn't too late.'

They agreed to meet in the terminal in 45 minutes.

Tomlinson wanted to speak to Joe Patroni and the airline employees from Flight Two. Mel supposed that they would be the heroes of his story – not Mel and his dry information about airport management. But the young reporter would write a good and fair story, Mel was sure of that.

He watched as the undamaged Aéreo-Mexican plane was moved away, to be washed and checked before it flew again.

There was no reason for Mel to stay on the airfield now, but somehow he wanted to.

Only a few hours ago he had felt that something terrible was about to happen. It had happened, although it had not been as bad as it might have been. But unless the airport changed, and changed quickly, something much worse would certainly happen.

Lincoln International was out of date. It was well managed, had fine buildings and was used by thousands of people, and yet it was hopelessly out of date.

Much had been said about the future growth of aviation, and not enough had been done. Mel knew that he must say what he thought about this. He had only one voice, but it would be heard.

He would begin by calling a meeting of the Airport Committee. He would tell them how important a new runway was, and that what had happened tonight had shown him how badly it was needed. If they did not agree with him, he would fight them as hard as he could, and he would make sure that the newspapers and the public knew all about what was happening.

People who thought that Mel Bakersfeld was finished were about to discover their mistake!

Tomorrow he would move into a hotel. It would be an unhappy time, and he hoped that neither Roberta nor Libby would see him go. Later, he supposed, he would get an apartment of his own. He knew that he would never live with Cindy again.

And Tanya? He was not sure yet what would happen. He knew that tonight he had needed the comfort of her friendship, but he did not know whether their relationship would be short or would last for many years.

Other planes were now beginning to use runway three zero, arriving in a steady stream in spite of the late hour. As one landed, Mel could see the landing lights of another flight coming nearer, and a third beyond that. The fact that he could see the lights of the third plane made him realize that the clouds had gone. He noticed suddenly that the snow had stopped falling. 'At last,' he thought. 'The storm is moving on.'

ACTIVITIES

Chapters 1–8

Before you read

1 List as many people as you can who work at an airport. What do you think are the problems and satisfactions of their jobs?
2 Check the meaning of these words in your dictionary. They are all in the story.

air hostess   agent   aviation   calendar   cigar   conscience
divorce   maintenance   runway   sigh   snowplough
stowaway   terminal   truck

Read the clues and complete the crossword puzzle with the new words.

Clues across

1 a thing that people smoke
4 an unsuccessful marriage may end in this
5 a sad person may make this sound
7 she serves food and drinks to aeroplane passengers
9 a table showing the days, weeks and months of the year
10 this tells you if something is right or wrong
12 a person who represents a company
13 the surface, like a road, on which planes land and take off

Clues down

2 the science or practice of flying
3 building in which people wait for planes, buses, ships, etc.
5 use this to clear snow off the road
6 regular repairs to a machine
8 a person who hides on a plane or ship to avoid buying a ticket
11 a large road vehicle

After you read

3 Explain why:
   a runway three zero cannot be used.
   b there are crowds of people inside the airport terminal.
   c the airport is receiving complaints from Meadowood.
   d Mel is rarely eager to go home.
   e Patsy throws a book at a passenger.
   f Joe Patroni's progress to the airport is slow.
   g Vernon is looking forward to his stay in Italy.
   h Mel can no longer fly planes.
4 What are the relationships between:
   a Mel and Vernon?
   b Mel and Keith?
   c Mel and Tanya?
   d Mel and Cindy?
   e Tanya and Patsy?
   f Vernon and Gwen?

125

5 Patsy throws a book at a difficult customer. Discuss other ways of dealing with rudeness in work situations. Try them by acting out conversations in pairs between an awkward customer and a ticket agent at a ticket desk.

Chapters 9–16

Before you read

6 List the problems facing Mel Bakersfeld both professionally and personally. Which problems are easier to solve? Which are more difficult?

7 Find these words in your dictionary:

abortion   airline   chairman   parachute   policy   radar

Circle the correct word to complete each sentence below.

a The .... system showed the position of the aeroplane.
  (i) radar
  (ii) airline

b The .... of the company made all the important decisions.
  (i) policy
  (ii) chairman

c We chose to travel with an independent .... with a good record for safety and efficiency.
  (i) parachute
  (ii) airline

d After her husband died, Mrs Crane collected money from his insurance ....
  (i) policy
  (ii) chairman

e Because of medical problems, Mrs Jackson had to have ....
  (i) an abortion
  (ii) radar

f The aeroplane was in trouble. The captain told the passengers to put on their ....
  (i) policies
  (ii) parachutes

After you read

8 Answer the questions.

   a Why is it important for the air traffic controller to clear a path for Air Force KC-135 to land?

   b Why do you think Elliot Freemantle is such a success at the Meadowood meeting?

   c What is D. O. Guerrero's plan?

   d Why is Joe Patroni angry with the police?

   e What is Vernon surprised about in Gwen's apartment?

   f What news does Gwen give Vernon at the apartment? How does he feel about the news?

   g What is the importance of the key in Keith's pocket?

   h What help does Tanya want from Ada Quonsett?

   i Why is Cindy planning to come and see Mel at the airport?

   j What was the reason for Mel and Vernon's big argument? Who won?

9 Describe the air traffic radar room in which Keith works.

10 Describe Keith's plan and explain the reasons behind it.

Chapters 17–24

Before you read

11 What preparations do you imagine are made before a plane is ready for passengers to come on board?

After you read

12 What do you know about the *Golden Argosy*?

   a Which airline owns the plane?

   b Where is it leaving from and where is it going to?

   c Which gate do passengers leave from?

   d Who is flying the plane? Who is with him at the plane's controls?

   e Name one of the air hostesses on the flight.

   f Why is the flight delayed?

   g What does it fly over immediately after take-off?

   h Which passenger's name does not appear on the passenger list?

   i Which passenger has no intention of completing the journey?

13 If Guerrero succeeds, what are the police likely to find out about his movements before he boarded the plane? Who should they interview?

14 What do you think Gwen and Vernon will decide about their baby? What decisions do you think they should make?

Chapters 25–32

Before you read

15 Inez Guerrero is left sitting outside Mel's office by the police chief. What do you think she believes her husband is doing? What do you think she will do next?

After you read

16 Correct the statements that are false.
  a Mel is upset about losing Cindy.
  b Mrs Quonsett is about sixty years old and dressed in black.
  c Harris does not believe in abortion.
  d Ada Quonsett is sitting behind Guerrero.
  e Mel becomes very angry with Elliott Freeman.

17 Answer these questions.
  a What facts do the airport team discover about Guerrero to worry them?
  b How does the Aéreo-Mexican pilot make Joe Patroni's job more difficult?
  c Why does Ordway think Bunnie was crazy to sell Guerrero an insurance policy?
  d What does Inez tell Ordway that makes them sure Guerrero has a bomb?

18 Describe Vernon's plan and what happens when they try to carry it out.

Chapters 33–41

Before you read

19 What do you think happens in the plane as a result of the bomb going off?

After you read

20 Correct this paragraph to describe how the story really ends. Guerrero's bomb blows a hole in the side of the plane, killing Gwen and injuring others. Vernon takes the plane down to ten thousand feet so that the passengers can breathe. At the airport, Mel fails to persuade the people of Meadowood to go home. He urgently needs to clear the blocked runway so that the plane can take off. The plane that is stuck is pushed to one side with snowploughs just in time. Keith is too upset to guide the *Golden Argosy* down, but it lands safely.

21 How does the story end for:
   a Mel and Cindy?
   b Gwen's unborn child?
   c Keith?
   d Joe Patroni?
   e Mel and Tanya?

22 Discuss which characters have grown stronger as a result of this terrible night, and how this is shown in the story.

Writing

23 Write a newspaper report describing how Joe Patroni managed to clear the runway.

24 Imagine that you live in one of the Meadowood houses. Write a letter of complaint to the airport authorities, and propose a solution to the noise problem.

25 Describe what happened on the *Golden Argosy* after the explosion, from the point of view of one of the passengers.

26 Write the letter that Guerrero wanted to write to his wife, explaining why he feels that his plan is necessary.

27 Compare the different relationships between men and women in this story, and the reasons why they work or fail.

28 Discuss Mel Bakersfeld's view that it is perhaps better not to know about an airport's dangers and weaknesses.